COVERT COUGAR CHRISTMAS

TERRY SPEAR

Discover more about Terry Spear at:
http://www.terryspear.com/

ISBN: 1633110230
ISBN-13: 978-1-63311-023-6

DEDICATION

To fans of the Yuma Town Cougar site that comment so diligently: Jonette En Vida, Linda Amirkhizi, Sarah Fisher, Carrie Summers, Tonya McClinton Kaelin, Susan Sleath Burgdorf, and Linda Boulanger!

Thanks so much, ladies!!!

ACKNOWLEDGMENTS

Thanks to Donna Fournier for all her help in brainstorming and editing. I couldn't have done it without her. And thanks to the individuals who are role playing with the Yuma Town cougars and having a blast! I have fun reading the mischief they get into without my help. And I can't wait to write their next stories: Dan and Dottie's, Stryker and...hmm, whoever the mystery woman of his dreams, or...nightmares, shall be.

CHAPTER 1

Snowflakes and ice drizzled down his windshield as Travis MacKay hoped the winter storm warnings and winter weather advisories for later this week weren't wrong and the storm was coming in earlier than expected. His Dodge Durango slipped on another patch of ice, and he tightened his hands on the leather-covered steering wheel. He was in a real time crunch already if he was going to pack and move his household goods from Cheyenne, Wyoming to Yuma Town, Colorado before the weather worsened and before New Year's Day at the latest, when the new owners moved in.

It was nearly two in the morning when he reached the outskirts of town and realized he needed groceries and packing boxes. He was certain some grocery store would be open this late and drove into town, but found that none of them were. Then he spied several bundles of great, clean boxes folded and tied up next to a Dumpster behind a Christmas pop-up store, set up for business only during the holidays. Packing boxes had been another of his pressing priorities to get first thing in the morning and he was delighted to check one thing off his list. He pulled into the alley behind the building and parked.

He got out of the car, but out of the corner of his eye, he caught sight of something move. He spun around to see if it truly was what he thought he saw. A golden cougar! Beautiful. The cougar raced past the entrance to the alley. A female, or younger male, not as big as an adult male.

A shifter like him? He couldn't imagine it was a full cougar. Not in town like this. Yet he had never run across a shifter in Cheyenne before. Because of his cat's curious nature, it made him want to chase after the cougar and learn the truth.

But he was now working out of Yuma Town as a field agent of the Cougar Special Forces Division, CSFD that took down rogue cougars.

Still, Travis took another long look in the direction the cougar had run, and hoped the cat would return so he could get another look at it when he knew it wouldn't come back. The cat would think Travis was human and a real danger because he might call the sighting into animal control and someone would come out and shoot the cougar.

Then he saw the Christmas shop's back door propped open. He was going to holler out that he wanted to use the boxes for moving if that was all right with the shop owner, but heard a heated argument inside, and paused. He listened in case he needed to stop a fight. Being a Ranger with the army and well trained in tactical maneuvers in his current job, Travis was well qualified to intervene and break up a fight, when he heard one of the men arguing say, "What do you mean that bastard wants more money?"

"He said if we don't pay up, he'll shut us down permanently. And I don't mean that we'll have a chance to pull up stakes and start up our operations someplace else in the States either."

"Then we need to take *him* out."

"Yeah, right. The two of us against—" The man abruptly quit talking.

His heart thundering in his ears, Travis backed toward his car as quietly as he could, but his boot crunched on frozen snow. He pulled out his Glock, ready in case anyone came out of the building with a gun trained on him.

"So how much did we make on sales today?" the one man asked as if there was nothing the matter.

"Fourteen hundred and some pocket change. So not too bad. The angels are really going over big this year. And the naughty elf wooden ornaments from Denmark too."

The other man chuckled. "Our Christmas trees are making the real money. Can you give me a hand with setting up another couple of trees where sales have left some bare spots?"

"Yeah sure."

Travis hesitated. His kind didn't take down human criminals, unless a situation presented itself and he couldn't avoid it. If the men were cougars, different story. It sounded like the men were up to no good, but without some kind of evidence to go by, he couldn't alert the police. And he couldn't go in to check and see if they were cougars either. First thing in the morning when the shop was open, he could sniff around. Or later, when the men went home, he could check out the boxes and see if they smelled like cougars had touched them.

He eyed the pristine boxes one last time, wishing that everything had been on the up and up, and he could have just gotten the boxes and been done with it.

Then Travis saw movement out of his peripheral

vision. Instinctively, he lunged to the right, hoping he was overreacting, but if not, that his car would give him cover, hating that it could be shot up though.

A blond-haired man was armed with a rifle and fired a shot. Travis's quick reaction hadn't been fast enough. The shooter had been just as quick, like a highly-trained sniper.

Travis heard the shot fired, felt the stick of a dart when it hit his shoulder, and he yanked it out. By the time he fired his own gun at the shooter, Travis was sinking to the asphalt, cursing himself all the way down. His vision blurring, he hoped to hell his shot had impacted on the guy's body somewhere that it would make a difference. His mind drifting, Travis reminded himself there were two men, not just the one. And then his world faded from gray to black.

***

Bridget Sinclair was certain the two men who had opened the Christmas Tree Shoppe, were using the store as a front for criminal activity. The director of the CSFD, Chuck Warner, had given her the assignment after an informant had said there might be a connection between these men, Heaton Sadler and Franklin Dewitt and another, who demanded protection money so they could launder drug money. If she found there was anything to the allegation, she was supposed to call for backup before she took action. She prowled around the front of the shop in her cougar form. It was easier for her to disappear at this time of night as a cougar. No one would be able to identify her human-wise, and she was wearing hunter's spray to disguise her scent. She assumed that no one would be at the shop this late. It was two in the morning, a small light on in the building casting ghostly shadows on the trees, making it look like a haunted Halloween store instead of a cheery Christmas tree store.

She might be new to the business of being a special agent with the cougar police force, but she'd been a Special Agent with the Criminal Investigation Command in the army. The difference between this job and that had been that she had investigated serious and felony cases in the army, but couldn't arrest anyone. She loved being able to do both. Besides, she really wanted to take down bad cougars who could ruin it for the rest of them.

She headed around back and saw a bright red Dodge Durango parked there, Colorado plates though. The men she was after were from Florida. Then she saw a black-haired man in front of the vehicle, who suddenly turned when she caught his eye.

Heart thundering, she raced off, cursing herself mentally. She hadn't wanted these men to see her in any way, shape, or form. A shot rang out and she leapt into some tall juniper shrubs, certain that the man had run down the alley and taken a shot at her.

But when she peered out, she saw a blond-haired man, rifle in hand, and recognized him as Heaton, before he ran into the alley. She assumed then that he had shot the dark-haired man near the parked vehicle. She listened with her psychic senses, trying to hear anyone's thoughts, but she was too far away. She ran back toward the alley, and chanced peeking around the wooden fence separating it from a housing development. Heaton and a redheaded man she recognized as Franklin, also armed with a gun, were peering down at the man Heaton must have shot, now lying in a heap on the asphalt.

Was the dark-haired man innocent? Or just one of their men that they'd had a disagreement with? She hugged the fence as they dragged him into the Christmas Tree Shoppe. Alive? Dead? She didn't see a blood trail. The breeze was blowing in the wrong direction for her to get a whiff of blood or of any of the men's scents.

If he was innocent of any wrongdoing and he was still alive, she had to rescue him. If he was guilty, she still needed to save him, *if* he was alive, and she would force him to tell her the truth about the criminal operations as far as he knew about them.

She'd seen no other vehicles around, so she assumed Heaton and Franklin had a place nearby, had walked to the shop, and that the vehicle sitting there was the injured or dead man's. They would need another vehicle so they could dispose of the man's car and his body.

After a few minutes, Heaton and Franklin came out of the back door and walked past the parked car. She hid behind the fence and slipped into the thick junipers again.

"He had a Glock," Heaton said. "Fired the damn thing at me too. If it wasn't that the tranquilizer acted so fast, he might have hit me."

Tranquilizer? Thank God. Her heart was beating up a storm. She desperately wanted to reach the drugged man before they returned for him.

"So who the hell is he?" Franklin asked.

"I don't know. I thought he was one of Rambo's men. But if he had been, he would have just stormed right in, gun readied to take us out."

They headed toward the end of the alley in Bridget's direction.

Great. She needed to shift and try to rescue the tranquilized man before the rogue cougars returned. If they lived really close, that wouldn't give her much time. She raced back to her car parked three blocks away. Upon reaching it and hidden by the carport, she shifted in the bitter cold of the night, the stars twinkling against a black sky. *Cold, cold, cold.* Shivering, she put in the code to unlock her car, climbed in, shut the door, and quickly dressed. She considered taking her neon green Honda Fit, but was afraid it was too showy, risking jeopardizing her undercover mission, and didn't have enough get up and go to evade anyone who might take chase.

Armed with her 9mm and her Swiss Army knife, she raced back to the store, hoping she could disarm an alarm if the owners had set one.

She reached the back door, picked the lock, and was relieved no alarm sounded inside the shop. Probably because the cougars were conducting illegal business and they didn't want the police investigating a break-in. Especially when they had a drugged body in their shop.

Except for a small light on in one corner of the store, it was dark. She moved quickly through the decorated Christmas trees, their sparkly lights all off, the fragrance of cinnamon candles and pine scent filling the air. When she reached the checkout counter, she smelled the three men, all cougars, and heard snoring in a back room.

Her heart thundering, she swiftly opened the door to the room, 9mm in hand, and peered in. Though cougars could see at dusk and dawn, the room was pitch black. She pulled out her cell phone to give her a little light and saw the dark-haired man, probably six-feet, one in height, wrists bound with rope, duct tape covering his mouth. He appeared sound asleep.

Adrenaline pumping through her veins, she was desperate to get him up and moving with all haste.

She stalked toward him, thinking he could be a rogue cougar just like the others, and she might very well have to take him down too. She also figured she had an opportunity here. Take this guy with her and force him to rat on the others. Yet, neither Franklin nor Heaton seemed to know him.

"Come on, get to your feet," she said to the man, her words hushed but stern, assuming Heaton and Franklin would return to dispose of him before the shop opened at ten.

He groaned and opened his eyes, and then they widened. He struggled to get free.

"Listen," she said. "These men intend to kill you. I'll take you somewhere safe. But you have to do as I say. You tell me all you can about the guys, and we'll go from there."

He nodded vigorously. She didn't trust him in the least, but he probably assumed she'd be easier to take down than the men coming back for him. She tried to read his mind, but she couldn't, like a brick wall was blocking her penetration. Maybe it was due to whatever drug they'd doped him with, but even so, she expected to read some jumbled thoughts. Not that she could read everyone's. But most. Sometimes that got her into trouble.

She shoved her phone in her pocket and helped him to stand. "Is that your car out back?"

He nodded again.

"Okay, we'll get in it and drive away from here because mine is too far away for you to travel like this."

He nodded, but then tried to speak.

"When we get into your vehicle, you can tell me your story."

He tried to talk again, motioning with his body to a cabinet. Thinking there might be evidence inside, she leaned him up against a table and opened the cabinet. A Glock was sitting on one of the shelves. She looked back at him. "Yours?"

He nodded. She shoved it into her shoulder holster under her jacket.

He was so groggy that by the time she got him outside, she was afraid she wasn't going to get him to his car in time. She eyed the Christmas wreath attached to the grill of the Durango, either part of the Christmas Tree Shoppe cover he was using, or he was really a nice guy, a mated cat, and his wife hung it there.

He kept stumbling, and she was holding onto him with all her strength, but he was about a half a foot taller than her and weighed quite a bit more, muscle weight though.

He mumbled the car code to her and said something about keys, pocket, and she leaned him against the car, then hurried to put the code in.

Searching for his car keys next, she shoved her hand in his right jacket pocket and found nothing.

"Jeans," he said sleepily against the tape covering his mouth.

Feeling practically feverish with concern, despite the bitter cold whipping around her, she reached under his jacket and slid her hand down into his right front jeans pocket. No keys, damn it.

"Other," he mumbled.

As much as she knew this could be a bad guy, and that she shouldn't be thinking of anything other than grabbing the keys before they both got caught, she couldn't help feeling like she was groping the guy, her cold hand sliding into his warm pocket, brushing against his hot, muscular thigh. Then a modicum of relief washed over her as she felt his keys and struggled to get them out of his jeans pocket. She heard a car engine rumbling a ways off, but heading in this direction. Damn, damn, damn!

It didn't mean it was them, but she couldn't risk that it wasn't.

"That might be them coming." She opened the guy's passenger door, but he was having such a time trying to climb in with both his hands tied behind his back and the drug working against him, she was tempted to remove the bindings. Which could be a fatal mistake on her part. She had to give him credit for trying so hard to get into the vehicle.

She was attempting to help him into the Durango, and finally pushed his nice firm butt up to give him a lift. He fell heavily onto the seat. Relieved, she slammed the door, then bolted for the driver's side. As soon as she was in, she jammed the key in the ignition. Turning the engine on, she slammed her foot on the gas and tore off, glad it had a higher powered engine than her car. She charged out of the alley and around the corner, and kept on going. If the car approaching the alley had seen them leaving the alley, she didn't want them to catch sight of where she was now headed.

The guy in the seat next to her mumbled something about his house.

"Do they know where your place is located?"

He shook his head.

She reached over and tore the duct tape free from the side of his mouth, but couldn't pull it off all the way from where she was seat belted in and the tape still clung to the other side of his whiskers.

"Who are you?" he asked, his words still sounding drugged.

"Where's your house?" she asked, needing to get his vehicle out of sight pronto. She hoped he had a garage and he didn't have a bunch of villains living with him there. "And who are you, exactly?"

"I'm Travis MacKay. I don't know who those men are. Are you with a police force? We can't leave now. We need to take them out."

"Who's we? You couldn't shoot worth a darn in the condition you're in. Not that I trust you anyway."

Travis let out his breath. "I saw the bundled boxes out back of their shop and since they were clean, I figured I'd use them to pack my household stuff." He still sounded dazed, trying to get the words out as fast as he could.

"Moving, eh?" It sounded like a story to her. She took in a deep breath of the Durango's interior, new leather, the hot cougar, and the sweet scents of Christmas in the back of his vehicle. Chocolate fudge, peanut brittle, brownies, peppermint patties, and more. She glanced over the seat to see if he had any packing boxes, though she didn't smell any cardboard. Instead, she got a glimpse of Christmas decorated boxes with ribbons and Christmas cards.

"Yeah, I'm moving to Yuma Town. Well, hell, if you're not going to go back and take them out, my place is about two miles from here. Go straight two blocks, and then take a left. I was a Ranger in the army. You can check with my boss. I'm one of the good guys."

"Oh yeah?" She cast a glance his way.

He cast her an elusive smile that said he wasn't all that angelic. "Yeah, just put in a call to Leyton Hill. He's my boss in Yuma Town. Or the director of operations, Chuck Warner."

She gaped at Travis, but he quickly told her, "Turn left there and go straight five blocks."

She turned the corner then said, "You know Chuck Warner?"

Travis studied her now and she let out her breath. "Do you have your phone on you?"

"Yeah. Car console."

She turned on his car phone, linking it to his Bluetooth and said she wanted to speak with Chuck Warner. If Travis was giving her the real story, she and he worked for the same agency. She was relieved she wouldn't have to kill him.

"Hey, Chuck, it's Bridget Sinclair."

"You're calling from Travis's phone. Did the two of you hook up to check out the Christmas Tree Shoppe?"

"Kind of." She smiled a little at Travis. She wondered how much it would be worth it to him to keep how she found him secret from the boss.

"I thought he was in Yuma Town still," Chuck said.

"He said he was getting ready to pack his household goods."

"Now?"

"Apparently." She glanced at Travis to let him tell his own story.

"Hey, boss. I've got to be out of there by New Year's Day. And with the winter storm approaching, I need to do this fast. But it looks like I've got a mission too," Travis said, still sounding drugged and half asleep.

"I've called Chet Kensington and he's on his way now. If you've got to pack up and move, no problem."

"No. I'll help Bridget. This has just gotten damn personal."

She raised her brows at him.

Travis smiled a little back.

"Good. Bridget's new at this, so I told her I wanted her to call for backup if there was anything to this business. I'm glad you're there. I'll get hold of Chet and tell him you'll be at your home until you have to leave. You... don't quite sound yourself. Are you okay?"

16

"Yeah, nothing that a good night's sleep won't cure. Got to let you go so I can keep giving Bridget directions to my house so the bad guys don't catch up to us."

"What the hell is going on?" Chuck asked.

"We'll explain after we hide Travis's vehicle. Got to go, sir," Bridget said, not wanting to miss any turns.

"All right. But I want word back as soon as you can call me."

"Will do. Out here." She smiled a little at Travis. "So, exactly how long have you been working for the agency? And what's your cover story for the director about what happened to you tonight?"

She was certain he wouldn't want to tell the director what had *really* happened to him. If the roles had been reversed, she certainly wouldn't want to be him.

"And what are we going to tell your wife when we get home?" she tacked on, not wanting to get into it with a growly she-cat either when they arrived at his place.

CHAPTER 2

Travis felt like shit. He could barely stay awake, while he breathed in deeply to smell the she-cat's scent. But she didn't have a scent at all. So was Bridget wearing hunter's spray?

Instead, the sweet aroma of the Christmas treats in the back seat wafted through the car. The lovely lady cougars of Yuma Town had worried he wouldn't have any time to celebrate Christmas when he returned home, but if he ate all of the goodies they sent with him, he was going to have to do a hell of a lot of running as a cougar to work off all those extra calories.

He guessed she thought he had a wife because of all the baked goods in the back. "No mate."

"Really?" She cast a quick glance his way, dark

eyebrows raised.

"Yeah, the candies are from mostly mated she-cats in Yuma Town."

"Oh. And the Christmas tree wreath on the front of your grill?"

He smiled a little. "The ladies in Yuma Town wanted to make sure I didn't miss Christmas, so they made up the evergreen wreath. The guys all gave me and their mates a hard time, and told me that they would understand if I ditched it the minute I left Yuma Town."

"But you didn't."

"Nope. When I drive back there, I'll be proudly displaying it through New Year's."

She smiled.

Travis thought Bridget was a first class agent. She was a beautiful brunette with her hair curling past her shoulders, her blue-gray eyes electrifying. When he'd first seen her, the cell phone light softly illuminating her, her pretty eyes considering him, he thought she was one of *them,* and he'd hoped he could convince her to take pity on him before the men came back to try to finish him off. They'd run off to some storage facility for tools or something to take care of him. So that was one of the things he and Bridget had to check on. Storage facilities all over Cheyenne to see if they had anything in one to prove their involvement in illegal activities.

But it had been a real effort on his part to try and tell her he was one of the good guys when she might have been with the bad guys when he was so groggy and the men had taped his mouth shut. When she said she wanted to know everything he knew about the suspects, he didn't know if she was playing him or what. He wasn't sure if she wanted to learn if he knew what their business was or if she truly was investigating them. As concerned as she was that she got him out of there before they got caught, he realized she had to be some kind of police official, undercover, he suspected, because she wasn't wearing a uniform. No way had he thought she'd be a special agent with the same agency he was with.

His director would have mentioned the case to him. Then again, Travis hadn't had time to tell him he was returning home this week to pack up.

He'd never thought he'd come home for his last time here and pick up a mission either. But working with her totally appealed. Even if she was a rookie. Hell, she did a damn good job saving *his* ass.

He guided her the rest of the way home, though twice she had to shove at his shoulder to wake him up. He hated that he was so out of it when she was so with it. But at the same time, he was glad she was able to get him out of the tight bind he'd been in. He still couldn't believe that spying some great boxes for packing his household goods could have led to his demise.

"Where's your garage door opener. Forget it. I see it." She poked the garage door opener and once the door opened, she quickly drove into the garage and shut the door.

"Were they following us?" He couldn't believe he was so out of it he couldn't even watch the mirrors to help out.

"No. Thankfully, they must have driven off the wrong way once we left the alley. You can't use your car now until after we take them down."

He hadn't been certain she'd want him for a partner. He was glad she did, even though she had no choice. He wasn't letting her do this on her own. Though they did have a problem. The men knew his scent, his car, and what he looked like in his human form. He could wear hunter's spray to disguise his scent at least and rent a vehicle, but he'd have to disguise his appearance.

"Where's your car and belongings?" he asked.

"My car is about three blocks from the shop. It's sitting in a guest carport at an apartment complex. I'm staying at a hotel because the director said he didn't have any safe houses in the area."

"Mine is one. I mean, it's mine. But I let other

agents stay here anytime they need to. I have three guestrooms to choose from. It would be better if you stayed here so we could work out a plan."

"Okay. I want to get my car now, but while there's not much traffic on the road, I should wait until a little later. You need to sleep off whatever drug they gave you." She went around to the passenger door, opened it, then used her knife to saw through his ropes.

"Agreed." Travis really hated that Bridget had to help him out of the car. He pulled off the rest of the tape from his whiskers. It stung like crazy and he was certain it yanked out a few of his whiskers. He was still feeling so loopy, he would have fallen on his face if she hadn't been there to halfway catch him. But she was a petite little thing and she didn't have the muscle mass to really stop him if he hadn't regained enough of his equilibrium to straighten himself out. They made it inside the house and he said, "Bedroom is down that hallway."

"Okay, I'll grab the rest of your stuff after I get you to bed."

He smiled a little, wishing she'd just curl up with him. Then he said what he was thinking out loud, trying for lighthearted and humorous when he still hoped she'd take him seriously and say yes! "Join me to watch over me, if you'd like."

She smiled at him, his arm draped over her shoulders. He really was trying not to lean on her, or stumble and fall. "Would you make the same offer to any of the other agents?" she asked.

He chuckled.

Somehow, he managed to collapse on the bed and the next thing he knew, she was removing his shoes, socks, and pants. A woman after his own heart if he'd been more with it. She slipped off his jacket, then his shirt, and considered him for a moment. He didn't think she was sizing him up as far as how sexy he looked, but trying to figure out how to get him under the covers. "I normally sleep in the buff."

His comment earned him a sexy smile.

She finally just grabbed hold of the comforter from the other side of the king size bed and pulled it over him. She slipped his Glock out from underneath her jacket and showed it to him. "I take it this is yours?"

"Yeah, thanks."

"You don't have a police badge?"

"No, undercover. Chuck wouldn't issue one to me."

"Okay, good, so the guys don't know that you're a Special Agent."

"No. But I'm sure they wondered why I was carrying a Glock."

"True."

"Can I have a kiss good night?" he managed to say.

She smiled. "I bet you don't ask the other agents that either."

He smiled, closed his eyes and imagined her kissing him, when he felt warm lips pressed against his and he smiled, but before he could reach for her, pull her close, and kiss her back, he passed out again.

***

Bridget had to admit she really felt bad for the guy. Maybe because she could see herself in his shoes—just coming across criminal activity in a perfectly innocent way and getting herself into a bind. She wasn't sure how much help he would be though since the men could identify him. Still, if he was a veteran agent, she assumed he'd be able to aid her. He was cute too. She suspected when he wasn't drugged, he could be a real threat to the bad guys. And dangerously sexy with regard to unsuspecting she-cats when he was on the prowl. She would never have expected him in his drugged state to offer for her to join him in bed, or to ask her for a kiss good night.

She headed outside to the garage and carried in his sweet treats and his bag and dropped off the treats on the kitchen counter, then carried his bag into his bedroom. She glanced around the master bedroom, saw a photo of what looked like Travis and his parents on a fishing trip at a river, and a copy of a book with the cover of a sexy Highlander in a kilt and a wolf, *Heart of the Highland Wolf*. She read the synopsis and smiled. A romance about Highland wolf shifters?

She returned to the kitchen and checked out the boxes of candy. The treats were homemade and each had a different she-cat's scent on them, individually wrapped in cute little Christmas boxes from snowmen to Santa Claus, and had little Christmas gift cards attached. She began to read the cards: Merry Christmas, Travis! A sweet treat to remind you of home. Love, Dottie. Best of the Holiday Season, Travis! Some sweets to give you energy to pack up and return home to your new family. Love, Shannon. Merry Christmas, Travis! I didn't want to be the only she-cat in town who didn't send you well-wishes and a treat! Love from Doc Kate. Happy Holidays, Travis! We expect you home for New Year's Eve, you hear? Love, Tracey.

Bridget wondered if one of them was his girlfriend since he'd said the women were *mostly* mated she-cats. He better not have a girlfriend and then want to sleep and kiss Bridget! She pulled out a piece of chocolate fudge. She sank her teeth into the chocolatey fudge delight, and groaned. This was an orgasm in the making.

She stared out the window, a security light partially illuminating the backyard, a forest of trees backed up on it. She desperately wanted to retrieve her car and grab her stuff from the hotel. But she knew it would be safer if she went when more people were up and about on the roads.

She finished the piece of fudge, then looked in each of the guest bedrooms and decided to stay in the one closest to the kitchen, all done up in blues and greens. Before she retired for the night, she watched out the front windows for a couple of hours, looking for any sign of anyone driving around the area, checking on Travis periodically to make sure he was all right. Tranquilizers like that could kill a cat. His heart rate continued to beat steadily in his sleep, so she felt he would be fine. She thought about his devilish smile, despite being drugged, when she had pulled off all his clothes but his briefs. He was one hunk of a male cat and she imagined what it would be like to be making love with such a hot-looking guy.

She sighed and continued to look out the windows.

Unable to stay awake and figuring the men had never learned where they had gone, she stripped out of her clothes in the bathroom, and took a quick shower, then returned to the guestroom wrapped in a couple of towels, one for her long hair, her clothes folded under her arm. She left her clothes on a chair in the guestroom, pulled off the towels, and climbed under the covers. She wanted to take down the bad guys in the worst way, but she had to sleep too so she'd be ready for them.

Later that morning before she was ready to get up, she woke to hear someone rummaging through the kitchen. Had to be Travis. She quickly dressed in her jeans and white tank shirt, left the bedroom, 9mm in hand, and headed for the kitchen.

She peered around the corner of the entrance to the kitchen and saw Travis, showered, shaved, and dressed. He was wearing jeans, a white tank shirt, and boots, a Glock in hand. He looked like a wide-awake, hot-shot agent this morning. And no less dreamy than when she'd seen him mostly naked in his bed last night.

He set his gun on the counter and smiled, then moved in close to her.

She should have stepped back and regained her space, but darned if the guy didn't draw her under his spell. Despite her cautious nature, she had the curiosity of a cat and waited to see what he intended to do.

He pulled her into his arms and held her close.

"You're even more beautiful than I dreamed you were. Thanks for the save last night."

She breathed in his washed male scent, the fragrance of limes and man and cat. But he was breathing her in every bit as much—the same fragrance of limes and all she-cat. His body was already reacting to hers, the heat escalating, the feel of his maleness rising to the occasion, pressing against her. Her body instantly responded, her nipples growing taut, her nether region aching for his touch.

She should have shoved him away when she didn't know him at all, but after last night, she couldn't see him as just another name on the roster of agents who worked for the agency. He was hot muscled flesh and fit so nicely against her body.

She tried to read his mind, but didn't have any success today either. So it wasn't because he had been drugged. She smiled a little at his compliment, wishing she knew exactly what he had been thinking. "I thought you were one of the bad guys. Imagine my surprise to learn you were with the same agency as me."

"Believe me, I can be bad to the bone."

She laughed, then she motioned to the fudge container. "I helped myself to one last night. Hope you don't mind."

"No, be my guest. I keep thinking how much I need to exercise off all those extra calories. Besides, you totally deserve it." He released his breath on a heavy sigh. "About...last night."

"You were drugged, half out of it. Don't worry about what you said or did. I've already forgotten it."

He cocked a black brow, his hands resting on her shoulders, his thumbs rubbing them.

"About wanting to sleep with me. That was the drug talking. And the kiss. Same thing," she said, when he seemed to be waiting for her to explain further.

He smiled. "Yeah, about that. I just didn't want you to get the wrong idea. I never ask agents to join me in bed or to kiss me."

She laughed again. He was so funny. "I'm the only female the agency has working for them."

"Well, there's that. But I just want you to know I don't pick up she-cats at Christmas Tree Shoppes in the middle of the night and take them home with me, normally."

She patted him on the chest. "Your secret is safe with me."

"What if I don't want to keep it secret? What if I want to kiss you back for saving me? I would have been a gonner if you hadn't."

"I was just being an agent and rescuing you, even

though I thought there was a good chance you were one of the bad guys."

"So then thinking so ill of me, maybe you'd like to kiss me to make up for it?"

She laughed again, leaned in to give him a kiss on the cheek, her breasts pressing against his hard chest, her face tilted up to his, when he moved his hands to her face. He held her as if he knew she only meant for this to be brief and not in the least bit intimate. Just a sweet thank you.

But he wasn't going for sweet.

His warm mouth pressed against hers, conquered and commanded. She wasn't one to back away from a challenge, not when she was feeling the draw to him like he was feeling toward her. It was a raw animalistic pull, like wild animals had. A sixth sense that told them that he was the kind of hot cat she could easily mate and have babies with that would have great genes from both of them.

Her hands slid around his back telling him she was in this with him all the way, her lips parting, inviting him to explore her, to deepen the intimacy. His hot tongue swept over hers, sliding, and teasing, his lips again kissing hers.

Their pheromones were out of control, hers, his, both triggering the other's in a hot mating dance, encouraging them to take this further. But their human halves, or at least hers, made her pull her mouth away from his, catch her breath, and wonder what the hell had just happened.

"I need to get going, get my car, and check out of my hotel," she said.

He resettled his hands on her hips, then kissed her forehead. "Okay." His voice was just as husky as hers.

She pulled away, feeling the urge to fan herself as hot as her blood was.

He leaned against the counter and folded his arms, his look intense. "I want to do this with you. I don't like it that you're out there on your own."

"I'll be super cautious."

"All right." He looked into a kitchen cabinet and closed the door. "Sorry. No fixings for breakfast or much of anything else. I planned to grocery shop today."

"I'll have to do it. You can't go out."

"Hell, we're going to have to take these guys down ASAP. There's no way I'm going to be stuck at the house, worried I might be seen."

"Okay, I'll do what I need to do. Then I'll come back here, and we can have breakfast and discuss it."

He pulled out his wallet and gave her a hundred dollars. "For the food."

"You don't have to—"

"After what you did for me last night? I owe you my life. Those guys meant business, and I aim to reciprocate. First thing tonight when it's dark out."

"What did you learn when you were at the shop? Anything?" she asked.

"Just that the two men were paying someone protection money."

"A cougar, you think?"

"Might be, or not. I smelled them in the store, but no signs of any other cougars." He took a deep breath of the air. "Not even you."

"I didn't want them catching my scent. I have to be able to move about them without them knowing I'm one of them. Listen, I've got to go. Anything you prefer to eat?"

"Just whatever you feel like. I'm easy."

"Good to know," she said, smiling. "You were really easy last night."

He chuckled darkly. "Next time, we'll be on more even footing. Let's exchange numbers just in case you run into trouble."

They did, and then she called for a cab and as soon as it pulled up, she was off, hoping that she wouldn't run into any trouble at the apartment complex where she had left her car. Or the hotel where she had left her suitcase. She had the cab driver pass by the Christmas Tree Shoppe and spied five vehicles parked out front. She had the cabbie drive her past the alley and saw a black pickup truck. She jotted the license plate down in her phone.

When the cabbie pulled into the apartment complex, she paid him and after he left, she headed around to another section of apartments where her car was parked. All this undercover, secret agent stuff was new to her. She usually just questioned friends and family of suspected army personnel involved in criminal activities, nothing covert about it.

When she turned on the car's engine, she got a call and took it on her Bluetooth link. "Yeah, Travis? Forget something you wanted me to pick up for breakfast?"

"Just checking to make sure you're okay."

"How sweet of you. I ran by the Christmas Tree Shoppe and caught the license plate number off a black Ford pickup if you want to check into it."

"Good job. Will do."

"At least five cars were parked out front. They have a sale on everything because it's so close to Christmas. Did you want anything?"

"No," he said emphatically.

"I'm going to stop in and see what they have."

"I'd rather we did it together."

"But they'd recognize you. I'm at my hotel. I'll

call back when I reach the grocery store and make sure I get what you want too. And then I'll let you know when I'm at the shop. I'll keep you on the line so you know I'm okay."

She didn't have to read minds to know he wasn't happy with her going it alone, considering what had happened to him in the dead of night. But she would keep him posted, just in case. "I'll be fine. I'm going in through the front lobby now." She had planned on ending the call, but she sighed, deciding to let him know she was fine all the way back to her car. When she was in her room, she said, "No one's been here other than a cleaning maid. I smelled her scent in the hallway so I know that's just her. Well, and other scents, but they're older. I'm going to take a shower, put on more hunter's spray and change clothes."

"Leave the phone on."

She laughed. "Why? So you can hear me sudsing up?"

"So I can hear you yell out if anyone tries to grab you. But yeah, if you want to tell me all about the delectable parts you're sudsing at the same time, that works for me."

She chuckled. "All right. This is weird, but all right. But I'm not giving you a play by play." She left her phone on the bathroom counter, locked the door, stripped, and showered. Then she dried off and sprayed hunter's spray on both herself and her clothes before she dressed.

She packed her bag, grabbed her phone, and headed down to the lobby. "On my way to check out," she told Travis.

"Thank you for humoring me," Travis said. "I've just contacted the sheriff's department in Yuma Town, all cougars, and they're investigating the license plate now."

"Wow, that's fantastic." She finished going over her bill and headed outside to her car, watching, making sure no one was following her. Then she used her GPS to locate grocery stores and drove to the nearest one.

"What are you driving?"

"Neon green Honda Fit." Bridget smiled when he didn't respond. "I know it's not a great getaway car and it's not inconspicuous, but when I bought it, I had no idea I'd be working for a secret cougar policing organization. So this is how I operate. Nobody would dream of me being a super special agent—cougar variety. Although, I will admit I didn't want to use my car to rescue you. I was hoping the Durango out back was yours. I was afraid my car would have been way too recognizable and it doesn't have a lot of power, so no get up and go."

"You need something with a lot more power

under the engine."

"Maybe later."

When she arrived at the grocery store, she picked up what he would like and what she wanted, and then made one last stop at the Christmas Tree Shoppe. "Okay, I'm at the shop. There are seven cars here now. I'll keep talking to you while I'm in the shop, asking what you'd like for our tree."

"If you have any trouble, you scream your head off and I'll be there in a heartbeat."

"I can do that. Okay, honey," she said, changing her tone from impersonal to something much more personal. "I just walked into the Christmas store, and I know you didn't want to come with me, but since it's our first Christmas together, can you tell me what you would especially like on our first tree?"

Nine women were shopping in the store, two with pre-school age children, and a blonde woman in her early twenties was at the checkout counter ringing someone's purchases up. Bridget didn't see any sign of the two men who had left their scent in the store. So maybe the black pickup truck out back belonged to the clerk.

"Oh, honey, I found just the ornaments for you and me. I'll just leave it as a mystery. Can't wait to show them to you." She picked out a boy and girl naughty elf wood carved ornaments and then a couple of angels. She took them to the checkout counter and smiled at the clerk. "How long will you have the sale on for?" Bridget pulled out cash and paid for her purchase.

"Through New Year's."

"Thanks! I'll be sure to come back." Then Bridget left with the sack in hand, telling Travis he was going to just love the ornaments she got for him.

"Let me guess. Angels for me and naughty elves for you."

She closed her gaping mouth. Did he have psychic abilities? Is that why she couldn't read his thoughts? Then how could he read hers? "How did you know?"

He laughed. "Because that's what I overhead the men talking about. Those two items were their bestsellers. I figured that they just said so to make it sound as though they had gotten over their disagreement, but in truth, they were planning to ambush me."

"Oh. Well, yes, and no. That's what I got, but I thought you'd get more of a kick out of the naughty elves. Somehow, I don't see you as being the angel type. Uh-oh, I've got a tail. I'm not going straight to your house."

"I'm coming to you."

"No, wait. I think...I think it's Chet Kensington.

Do you know him?"

"Yeah, darn good agent. What's he doing here? Are you sure it's him?"

"Yeah, incoming call from him. I have one more stop to make. I'll let you go so I can talk to him." She hung up on Travis and said, "Chet, so the director sent you?"

"Hey, Bridget, yeah. Are you going to Travis's place? Boss said he was moving."

"He had room for me."

"I wonder if he has room for me."

"I don't know. You'll have to ask him. I thought the boss was telling you that Travis would work with me on the mission."

"He did call, but I was already on my way here with only an hour or so to spare. I figured I'd drop in, see if I was needed, and if not, head on out."

She hated to say so, but she really did think he was needed, what with the rogue cougars already identifying Travis. She figured they could talk about it over breakfast. She had one more errand to make before she headed for Travis's place though.

"He's got a carport around back. That's where we always park when we use his place as a safe house."

"All right. So you know him pretty well?"

"Yeah. We've teamed up on a few missions. He's

really good at his job."

"Okay, good." She picked up boxes being discarded at a stationary store, then continued on her way to Travis's house. The homes were spacious and were situated on at least five-acre treed lots. She drove down the side driveway of Travis's place and parked around back where the carport was, hidden from the street. He had a forest of trees behind his place, and she thought how perfect it was for a cougar family. Had he sold it to one? Or just plain humans? It would be a waste if it just went to humans, she thought.

Chet pulled up beside her and got out. She was glad that he didn't grab his suitcase and assume that it was all right with Travis that he stay here too. And he was nice enough to help haul in the groceries.

Travis headed outside to help also, and slapped Chet on the shoulder. "Good to see you again." Then he moved around to her trunk to grab a bunch of groceries.

She was pleased to see him act friendly toward Chet and not all alpha posturing over his territory. To her, that meant he was a true alpha, not needing to claim his territory, or prove anything to another alpha. And Chet was totally an alpha. She had to let him know several times that she could handle things on her own during the last assignment they'd been on together. Sure he was being protective of her because she was new on the job, but she suspected it also had to do with her being a woman.

Chet's thoughts were all over the place too. From glad to see Travis, to wishing he hadn't been here so he could do this mission alone with Bridget. He was really nice, and he was really interested in her, but she never felt any spark between them. She wondered if she had been groping in his pockets for a pair of keys or stripping him out of his clothes, would she have felt anything between them? Maybe. But she didn't think so.

"You got boxes too," Travis said, sounding delighted.

She was glad she had made the extra stop now. "I can get you some other sizes, but I figured these would get you started. They're from a stationary store that was getting ready to trash them. And lots less dangerous to take off their hands than the ones at the Christmas Tree Shoppe."

"You can't know how much that means to me."

She could tell just from his cheerful expression.

"So," Chet said to Travis as they hauled in all the groceries and started putting them away, "tell me to get lost if you can't manage any more guests with packing or you really think you can handle this matter without me and I'll be on my way."

"Let's discuss it over breakfast," Bridget said.

Chet smiled. "That'll work for me."

Travis let out his breath. "They made me. It's been killing me to know Bridget is out there on her own after the two men got the best of me and planned to eliminate me."

She was surprised Travis had come out and spilled the beans about what had to have been an embarrassing situation for him. Yet, not once had he acted embarrassed about it. Just ready to take the criminals down.

Chet looked from Travis to Bridget and to Travis again, as if he couldn't believe he wasn't just joking. "I...take it you didn't tell the boss. He didn't say anything to me about it."

"I haven't talked to him. I've been on the phone all morning with Bridget, making sure she was okay." Travis eyed the red and white snowflake bag and smiled. "Can I see the ornaments you got for us?"

She felt her face flush with heat. She hadn't planned for Chet to be around to see them. "Sure." She finished putting away the food that needed to go in the refrigerator, then began making breakfast. She was trying not to pay any attention to the men as Chet waited for Travis to unwrap the tissue paper around the Christmas ornaments.

Travis unwrapped one angel, then the other.

Then he pulled out the next wrapped ornament and laughed. He unwrapped the second one and set them on the counter side by side. "These have to be mine."

She smiled. "I thought you'd like them."

They were primitives, round heads and oval bodies, stick legs and stick arms, round wooden noses, little red knit caps with tassels, but the female had round balls for breasts and the male had a woody between his legs.

Chet grinned. "I may have to get a couple of those myself."

"That's the shop we're investigating." Bridget started making pancakes.

"Where they grabbed you, Travis?" Chet asked. "Did you learn anything?"

"Just that they're paying someone protection money. They're using the store as a front," Travis said.

"The clerk was human. No sign of the two men who smelled like cougars. But now that they grabbed you and you got away, they might start using hunter's spray," Bridget said.

"Unless they believed I was just a cougar in the wrong place at the wrong time and they knew that I couldn't turn them into the police."

"True. But you had a gun on you."

"Agreed." Travis made a pot of coffee. "I got

word back on the truck's license plate number. It belongs to an Evie Lancaster. The interesting thing is I checked into a man named Rambo Lancaster a year ago. He shakes down businesses to offer them 'protection.' No Mob ties that we can tell. Just a low-life crook who makes big money off the little criminal entrepreneurs."

"Wait, Rambo? That's who they were talking about. No last name. Why don't you take him out?" Bridget asked.

"We have to concentrate on cougar shifter-related crimes. Shifters can't go to jail. That's why we have to deal with them instead of the police. I checked to see if Evie Lancaster is related to Rambo and she is. She's his daughter. So it looks like she knows how much they're raking in with their legitimate business, maybe how much they are getting in their drug sales, and how much they would owe for protection," Travis said.

"But the Lancasters are all human?" Bridget asked.

"Yeah."

"Does that mean someone on the police force is on the take?"

"Probably. But I checked. No cougars work at the police station, so whoever they are must be human."

She let out her breath in an annoyed way.

"Hey, I know how you feel. They all deserve to be taken down. But the regular police force needs to deal with it." Travis set the table, feeling like Bridget—that all of the bad guys needed to go down. But they really didn't have the manpower or resources to make it happen. "So if you had to kill someone, could you?" He still wasn't sure about having a woman in the agency. She might be a great investigator and a great shot with a gun, but if she had to take down a male cougar while in her cougar form, she'd be at a strong disadvantage.

"I could. If those men had returned to the shop before I was able to get you out of there, I would have had to resort to taking them out to protect both of us. No one would have stopped me."

"You could have left me there. You thought I was one of them, only I'd gotten myself in hot water with them and they were going to take care of me permanently."

"True. I did have it in mind that you'd be so grateful for my help, you'd tell me all about the operation."

"Disappointed?"

"Relieved. I would have broken my cover and if I'd let you go, then what? So I was glad you were one of the good guys."

"How are you going to change your appearance

so they don't know you if you try to work this investigation? Hey, I know. You could wear a Santa suit," Chet said.

Travis was going to say he would, if Chet went as his cute little elf's helper, but Bridget spoke first, and gave Chet a quelling look. "Yeah, you could, Travis. But *only* if you go shirtless and show off your hot abs. You could wear the boots, Santa's pants, a hat, and be one of those sexy Santas for grown-up parties."

Travis laughed.

But then they got down to business—how they were going to handle the rogue cougars.

CHAPTER 3

"We need to search storage facilities," Travis said. "They were going to get tools out of it to use to dispose of me."

"Right. And we need to look for the location where they had their vehicle. A house nearby? And then they walked to the shop?" Bridget served up pancakes and pork sausages. "They weren't gone for long from the time I saw them leave the shop to when they got their vehicle and returned."

"They were going to go to the storage facility before they returned." Travis took a bite of the blueberry pancake smothered in waffle syrup.

Chet was looking up something on his phone. "Three storage facilities are close to where the Christmas Tree Shoppe is located."

"Good. Then we need to check out the homes in the area close by and see if we can pick up their scents. Same thing with the storage facilities. They haven't been using hunter's spray so we might be able to catch them." Travis finished off his coffee and got a refill and filled up Chet's cup too.

"Tonight?" Bridget sipped her hot cinnamon tea. "Dusk is at five this evening. Should we run as cougars?"

"I think one of us should be driving and riding shotgun. If we run into other trouble, the cat or cats can get into the car, and we'll head home," Chet said.

"Or the cats can run home. Probably be less noticeable than a car driving along the road." Bridget buttered her pancakes, then poured maple syrup over them. "So what do we do in the meantime?"

"Do you want to take me to the shop and I'll pick up a couple of those ornaments?" Chet asked.

"You're kidding." Bridget looked like she didn't believe he really wanted some.

"No. We'll use it as a cover so I can check out the place. And the people."

"All right."

Travis finished eating his breakfast and offered to clean up the dishes. "I'll start packing while you're out. As soon as it's dark, I'm out of here." He wasn't going to sit at home while they solved the case.

Bridget smiled at him. "Well take a drive around the storage facilities and check them out. Maybe we'll get lucky and discover theirs and then return tonight to see what's in it."

"I just had a thought. If they do have some corrupt cops on the force, what if these guys have them run your license plate?" Chet asked.

"If they were going to do it, they probably would have come in the middle of the night to finish us off. They most likely don't want to do anything that would involve the police. Just as we don't want to get the police involved. Another thing—they might have assumed they were going to learn who you were before they got rid of you. They wouldn't have suspected anyone would come along and rescue you," Bridget said.

"What if they're spooked and take off?" Travis had worried about that, wishing he hadn't been so out of it, then he and Bridget could have waited for the men and taken them out when they returned to the shop.

"I wonder if the men only show their faces there late at night when the store is closed. Just set up more trees and such, do whatever other business they have to, but otherwise stay out of the public eye," Bridget said. "So that's their normal MO."

"Or the incident with me last night has made

them go into hiding like I'm doing."

"Then if that's the case, they'll be on the prowl tonight too, searching for you possibly. They didn't check your wallet, did they? See your driver's license? Your home address?" Chet asked.

"My wallet and phone were in the car's console. The alley was semi-dark, though as a cat I could see well. But as a precaution, when I left the vehicle I had my Glock on me and locked the car door before I went to get the boxes. The Durango was still locked when we went out to it."

"That could be why they hadn't moved it," Bridge said. "Did you want us to get more boxes for you while we're out?"

"Yeah. I'll probably need quite a few more."

"Okay, will do. Ready to go, Chet?" Bridget asked.

"Sure am. Don't work too hard, Travis. I don't envy you in the least."

Travis wished he was going with them, but he had to pack too, and he knew that his staying here was the safest bet for all of them. As soon as they left, he began taping up boxes and listening to the radio.

At once, the weather report caught his attention. Sleet was headed their way just about the time they were due to go out on their night hunt.

That would mean they'd have to run as cougars if it was too bad. Their paws spread wide to give them more balance and stability on ice and snow.

That meant no one would be riding shotgun tonight. And if the men were running around, they'd probably be in their cougar coats too.

***

Hell, he'd worked with Bridget on four jobs now and she was so hot, he wanted more. Her underneath him having the best sex of his life, or her on top, Chet was thinking.

Bridget and Chet were at the grocery store getting some more boxes, the weather worsening by the minute. Already the sleet was sliding down Chet's windshield and it was starting to stick to the cold pavement. They were rushing the boxes into Chet's vehicle before they got wetter.

She'd had enough. She'd begun to trust Chet, which was a mistake. He thought she did a great job while she'd worked with him on previous missions, and she appreciated that, but she had to tell him that his thoughts were getting in the way of keeping things between them professional. The more they worked together, the more he was thinking of how much he wanted her in bed. She just couldn't see him in that way. She really wanted to keep this on a strictly *special agent solving crimes* business.

"Quit it," she said harshly to Chet. She had to let him know the truth.

He glanced at her, looking puzzled.

"I can read your thoughts."

He smiled, like he didn't believe her. The few times she'd revealed the truth to someone, she found that was usually the initial reaction. People really couldn't read thoughts. At least most people she knew didn't believe in the ability.

Chet moved toward her, reaching out as if to pull her into a hug.

"Don't you dare," she growled. "I'm serious. I like working with you, but I'm not going to bed with you."

That took him aback. Now she read where he was wondering if his subtle hints hadn't been subtle enough.

"Okay, look, we have this chemistry between us and it's only natural for us to want something more." Chet obviously didn't believe her about her psychic abilities.

"No, there isn't. There's no chemistry at all." She climbed into the vehicle. "We need to hurry to the storage facilities now before it gets too icy." She knew there was no chemistry, not only because her thoughts kept returning to Travis and wishing he was here with her, but also when she was around Chet, her pheromones didn't spike. With Travis? They rocketed to the moon. And his pheromones reacted in the same way. Now *that* was animal chemistry. Their cougar halves dictated to them when they were interested, so it wasn't just a visual interest. And smells too. Travis had a hot, woodsy smell that made her think of fresh jaunts through the pines or spruce trees in a mysterious forest.

Chet wore a moldy leaf smell, a hunter's spray that would hide his cougar scent. It made her want to sneeze. Hers was scent-free.

"Don't tell me you feel something for Travis. You just met him. What? The fact you had to rescue him made you bond with him in some way? Hell, he should have been the one rescuing you."

She *did* feel a connection with Travis in that way, she had to admit. She'd saved his life. Somehow that tied them together in a way that went beyond anything else. Maybe it was because she couldn't read his thoughts, and yet, with him, she wanted to know just how much he'd love to have her in his bed! Even though she knew he did.

She sighed. They just had a raw, primal chemistry that sizzled between them. It was the only way she could explain it to herself.

"I like working with you, but that's as far as I want this to go between us."

"Have I said anything to make you feel threatened?"

He was analyzing his behavior, recalling the times he'd touched her, drawing into her space when he didn't need to.

"I can read your thoughts, Chet. For real. I know what you're thinking." Besides the way he was getting more and more into her own space, trying to push for something that wasn't there between them.

"Psychic? No way. I don't believe in that stuff."

She let out her breath. "Okay, think of something, anything."

His mind went blank.

"You're not thinking of anything. Just watching your driving."

"It's icy."

She folded her arms and was quiet, listening for his thoughts when he didn't feel pressured to think of something.

Then she read his thoughts about him seeing a psychic at a fair and the woman had told him he would marry a Chinese woman in Sacramento. Which was where the fair had been held.

"So the psychic was a fraud."

"What?" Now he sounded a little alarmed.

"The one who read your fortune in Sacramento? She predicted you'd marry a Chinese woman, but it didn't come to pass."

Chet's jaw dropped a little.

"Wait, there's one of the storage facilities."

He pulled in and they went inside a small office to talk to the owner of the facility. "Can we look around? I'm not sure what size I'll need," Bridget said.

"Sure. Here's a map showing the sizes, locations, and prices."

"Thanks." She and Chet headed through the gate and started smelling for any cougar scents.

"Does Travis know that you can read minds? Have you given him this speech too?" Chet asked her, his tone annoyed.

"No, and don't you tell him either. It's my business and when the time is right, I'll tell him. Besides, I can't read his thoughts." Though she suspected Travis was thinking the same things as Chet was concerning her. But at least she was feeling the same way about Travis.

Chet glanced at her.

She shrugged. "Sometimes I can't read people's minds. I couldn't read my parents'."

"What about the man in the office?"

"He was wondering if we were married and what we had to store."

"You could have guessed that."

"Yep, I could have." She really didn't care if Chet didn't believe her. She just wanted him to stop thinking such thoughts concerning her when he was with her.

"I don't smell any cougar scents around here, do you?" Chet asked and she was glad he was thinking about the mission.

"No. Let's check out the next one."

She returned to the office and said, "We're going to check out a couple of other facilities that are a little closer to where we live. But if we don't like what we see there, we'll be back."

"Okay. Thanks."

She left the map with the rental unit owner and then they returned to the car.

"So what was he thinking?" Chet asked as he drove off to the next facility, slipped on ice again, and cursed under his breath.

"I have no idea. I don't always try to read minds. I try to concentrate on the business at hand. I can block out the thoughts when I need to."

"But not my thoughts."

"I do, most of the time. But you're pushing it. Not just in your thoughts, Chet."

"All right, all right. Hell. I can't believe you read minds."

She smiled and settled back into her seat, then

began to worry again about the worsening weather conditions. By the time they reached the third storage facility, she hoped this was it because it was the only other one that was close enough for the men to have visited. Maybe they had only gotten their vehicle and hadn't gone to the storage facility first before they returned for Travis like they said they would.

As soon as they walked around the place, she said, "This is it." She was ecstatic and hurried in the direction she smelled that the two cougars had gone. They'd driven to a ten by twenty unit at the end of the facility. She smelled flakka. "Looks like we not only found the men's storage unit, but their drug stash."

"Sure wish we could call this into the police."

"After we take the men down, we can. Just hope that when we call the police, they aren't the ones on the take," she said.

They returned to the storage office, and they rented a unit as close to the rogue cougars' so they could return and break into the storage locker and make sure that the stash was in there. They bought a padlock from the owner, left a bolt cutter and backpack of clothing in their unit, and locked it. Chet would shift and dress and use the bolt cutter on the rogue cougars' lock, if he couldn't just drive there in his human form later tonight.

"What if we eliminated the men who put this here, then come back with a storage truck to move it?" Bridget asked as they headed back to Travis's place.

"Travis's rental truck? Then he'd be in trouble for hauling the contraband."

"What if we rented it in Rambo Lancaster's name?"

Chet smiled at her. "You know what Travis said about not going after humans."

"Right."

He laughed.

Cars were beginning to slide on the snow mixed with ice. One ran into a parked car, another tried to take a corner but ran into a stop sign instead. Everyone had slowed down to a crawl.

Travis called Bridget and she answered. "Yeah, we're almost home."

"How's the weather? I've seen two near accidents out front of the house already."

"Bad. We're going to have to run as cougars tonight. Hey, we're pulling in now. Good news. Share in a minute," she said.

When they arrived at Travis's home as icy as it was, it would be difficult to drive any vehicle tonight. They parked and Travis headed out to help them.

Thankfully, he had a covered walkway out to the carport.

She was all smiles when she exited the vehicle, thrilled to tell Travis the good news. Chet looked a little growly, probably because of her putting him in his place concerning their work relationship earlier, but with Travis, she was super friendly.

CHAPTER 4

To Travis's surprise, both Chet and Bridget helped him pack. He'd envisioned days of packing, but at this rate, the time would be cut in more than half. And it was fun. They had a couple of pizzas delivered and drank sodas, foregoing wine or beer because of the mission tonight.

"We couldn't locate their residence," Bridget said, writing on a box, then taping it shut.

"But the storage unit had a foul smell like sweaty socks. With our keen senses, we knew it was flakka, that new experimental street drug associated with bath salts," Chet said. "As long as it hadn't been stored there and then has been removed, Bridget had the notion of moving the goods and then destroying it or turning it over to the police."

"As long as we don't end up turning it over to the bad cops," Travis said. "You couldn't move the stash in a vehicle rented under your own name. If you got caught with it or police dogs smelled what you had transported...big trouble."

"What if we destroyed it right there in the storage unit?" Bridget asked.

"If we burned it, it could get out of control," Travis warned.

"So what? We just leave the alpha-PVP there?" Bridget sounded annoyed.

Travis shook his head. "But we have to do it right." He finished packing another box.

"What if after we take down the two men, we rent a vehicle with Rambo's name on it and move the stuff and then take it to a field to destroy it? Or, what if we steal one of Rambo's vehicles and haul the stash in it? Dump the contents, burn it, and return the vehicle before he's ever aware it went missing? We could hide evidence on the vehicle and then call the police. If we get hold of the bad cops, no big deal because the majority of the drugs would be gone. If we get hold of a good cop, then Rambo's in trouble."

"You're determined to take down humans in this venture," Travis said.

"He and the rest deserve to be."

"In your last job, you dealt with army servicemen that you were investigating. That meant humans. But in this job we go after cougars," Travis reminded her.

"The director wouldn't sanction us going after Rambo," Chet said.

Bridget grabbed another box and began wrapping glassware in linens. "I can't imagine doing this job right if we don't at least try to take down *all* the bad guys."

Travis finished packing another box and sealing it. "Okay, tonight we'll see if the men have left a scent trail from their home to the shop. As cats, we'll be able to tell better than when you were trying to drive by and still look inconspicuous. We'll concentrate on the two men who are cougars involved in criminal activities and who meant to kill me. We can decide what to do with the drugs after that." Travis looked out the window. "It's dusk. Time to get moving. We can't stick together, though I'd prefer it. But it isn't safe. We'll have to move separately so that no one will look out their windows and see three cougars looking suspiciously like they're amassing as if in a hunting party."

Chet looked at Bridget.

Yeah, that was what Travis was worried about

too. If she came upon two male cougars, she was going to be in trouble.

"But we're checking out the houses on the other side of the fence that's behind the alley to the Christmas Tree Shoppe first, right?" Bridget asked.

"Yeah. It's closest. Then we can check on the storage unit after that," Travis said. He got the directions for the unit in case he reached it first.

"I've got clothes at our locker." Chet gave Travis the combination for their lock. "And bolt cutters are in the unit if you get there before I do."

"Good thinking. Ready?"

Chet and Bridget nodded.

Travis wanted to tell Bridget not to take any unnecessary risks, afraid that she might feel she had to in order to prove she was just as competent as they were. She didn't need to prove anything to him. Not after she single-handedly rescued him. He was afraid if he told her not to take any unnecessary risks, she would be offended. So he did the next best thing.

"No heroics. We all need to return in one piece."

They both agreed with him and then Bridget returned to her room to strip, while Chet and Travis stripped among the boxes, and shifted.

***

Bridget hadn't wanted the men to treat her any differently than any other agent, so why did she slip off to the guestroom to strip and shift? Because she didn't want to hear Chet's thoughts on the matter. If it had been just her and Travis, she would have just stripped where he did.

Travis led the way because it was his territory and he knew it better than they did. She realized that once she left the woods and had to separate from the men, she felt more vulnerable. Not because she was a woman, but because she had envisioned doing more cougar work in the wild and not in more of a city environment. If anyone saw any of the cougars, they would call animal control and someone would be dispatched to shoot to kill. A cougar in a city could be bad news when it came to pets and small children. The cougars' presence in the city would signify the cougars were most likely hungry and looking for prey.

It was still sleeting and no one was travelling on the streets near where they were tonight, so the weather conditions couldn't have been more perfect for them. She saw Travis ahead of her when he went down the alley to the Christmas Tree Shoppe. She continued past the alley to the first street behind the fence.

Chet took the next street.

She hoped one of them would find the house where the men were staying. She just hoped Travis would let her and Chet know if he found the men at the shop and didn't try to take them out by himself.

Then she smelled the scent of the rogue cougars in this direction. Adrenaline shot through her blood, both with excitement mixed with apprehension and wariness. She headed for the one-story brick and siding house, watching for any sign of movement. The place had a light on somewhere in the back of the house. She mentally made a note of the address and drew close to the house. It was small, probably a rental, and the smell of the two men was all over the place. So she was fairly certain this was theirs. The Christmas Tree Shoppe was within walking distance.

She heard a voice speaking inside.

Were both men here then? Or just the one and he was speaking on a phone?

"Okay. Travis MacKay."

Her heart stuttered when she heard Heaton mention Travis's name.

Heaton stated Travis's address. "All right. This is the time to take care of him."

They must have had the crooked cop check out Travis's license plate number, and now they knew where he lived.

She was torn between taking this man out or getting hold of Travis. She weighed her options. Gun versus cat. Male cat versus she-cat.

She decided the only safe thing to do was go for Travis. She leapt over the neighbor's fence, hoping no one would be looking out at the pretty sleet. Then she raced across the yard and leapt over the eight-foot fence bordering the alley. When she landed on the asphalt, she saw no sign of Travis. *Great.* Had she missed him then? Had he taken off down another street?

She had to find him and Chet. She had to warn them that someone was likely coming for Travis at his house, and they had to prepare for it. Their guns and clothes were all at his house. And all three vehicles too. Damn it. Then all the men had to do was discover who their license plates belonged to.

She raced down the alley and out on the street, then headed past the street where the men lived, glancing in that direction, looking for a cougar. No sign of either Travis or Chet. She ran to the next street over, same thing. Then she did what she hadn't planned to do, warning the cougars in the house if they could hear her that she was out there. On the other hand, she needed to get hold of Chet and Travis before it was too late.

She let loose her most angry cougar gargling

growl, snarling, and hissing at the end. Her sounds could carry nearly a thousand feet. Hopefully one of the guys, the *good* guys, was within hearing distance.

But if the bad guys heard her? Then they could either be out to get her now in either their cougar form or armed with guns. They had to know there were at least two cougars, Travis and the one who had rescued him. Probably they'd figure another male had come to his rescue though.

She hid in tall junipers, waiting for someone to show up. Then she saw Travis!

She called out softly to him this time, more of a dark, low, rumbling purr.

He turned in her direction and bounded for the junipers she was hiding in. As soon as he was with her, he nuzzled her muzzle with his in greeting and as a well-being check. She did the same with him, so thankful that he had at least come, still worried about Chet. But they had to return to the house and be prepared. She shifted and shivered in the freezing cold, though the shrubs helped to protect her from the biting wind and sleet somewhat. "I just heard one of them talking," she quickly said. "One of the men at 1520. That's their house. He knows your name and your residence. He was telling someone that they'd have to do something, but not what. Move the drugs? Take care of you at your home? All our cars are there. And our clothes. Guns. IDs. Everything."

Travis shifted, pulled her into his arms, holding her tight to help warm her. "Okay. Where's Chet?"

"I don't know." Her teeth were beginning to chatter and she was shivering hard.

This was a difficult call. But if the men burned down Travis's home, they could destroy everything the three agents needed to take these men down as humans.

"Okay, let's go. If Chet heard you, he'll be headed this way, and he can follow our recent scents back to the house."

"Okay."

They both shifted into their cougar forms, the shift so quick that if a human saw them, he would think he'd been seeing things. Her body, muscles, and tissue warmed with the transition. They nuzzled each other one last time before they took off for the house.

They dodged through shrubs to give them some cover in the areas that weren't very treed. And finally, after what seemed like forever, they arrived at his house. No vehicles were parked nearby, and she was reminded that traveling on ice might preclude them from coming here that way. Which meant they'd arrive as cougars.

It also meant they could get in through the cat door because Travis had left it unlocked while they needed to use it.

They took in deep breaths of the area. They didn't smell any sign of anyone else, but if the guys were wearing hunter's spray, they wouldn't leave a scent unless they had been careless.

They listened, then Travis dove through the cat door. She waited a few seconds so if the men were inside, both she and Travis wouldn't be ambushed at the same time. She snarled and dove through the cat door and didn't see any sign of him. He had gone toward the bedroom, and then the door to the garage opened and a fully naked Heaton stood staring at her, jaw dropped, gas can in hand.

She leapt at him with one powerful jump and seized his throat before he could shift and tear into her with his mightier male cougar weight.

He fell back dropping the container of gas container and grabbing her by the neck to try and pull her off. She bit down hard, tasted blood, and wouldn't let go. Fighting for his life, he shifted. One moment his human's neck was between her teeth, the next, he was a blur and she had hold of a thicker, furry-necked cougar.

He was already too weak and she finished him

off before he could tear at her with his wicked claws. One last clamp down, and she heard his heartbeat slowing, then stop.

But what had happened to Travis?

She heard snarling in his bedroom, and she raced down the hallway to help him out.

***

Travis knew Bridget was fighting with a man, not another cat or he would have snarled right back at her. No shots were fired, so he assumed the man wasn't armed with a weapon. Probably hadn't been looking for anyone's guns. But the cat in here had been taking a dump in his bathroom, door locked, and Travis shifted to get his Swiss Army knife and unlock the door to get at the bastard, when he heard Bridget snarl. So did the man in his bathroom.

The bathroom had no window, and the man most likely wouldn't be armed. Instead he'd have to shift and take Travis on, but Travis wasn't waiting for the cat to get up the nerve. The rogue would have to open the door first and then shift, and he knew Travis could pounce on him and kill him before he managed to take Travis out.

This way, Travis was taking the risk, shifting into his human form, and then preparing for the man's pounce as a cougar. He could use his Glock. The guy had broken into his house with malicious intent.

Travis was perfectly in his rights to kill him using his gun.

He sure as hell didn't want to give this guy the advantage again.

Travis went for his gun, then unlocked the door, hesitated, then pushed the door open, and instantly took the stance to fire his weapon.

The growling cat lunged at him. Travis got off two rounds before the cougar took him down. Unable to use the gun on him now, though Travis smelled blood and knew at least one of the rounds had hit the bastard, Travis shifted and came up snarling, viciously tearing at the other cat, his teeth sinking into his neck and he held on, fishhook-claws digging into the cougar's shoulders, while the man tried in vain to wrench free.

Bridget snarled, coming to his aid, and Travis bit the man with one last final bite that took him out. He released him, listened for any sign of a heartbeat, faint, then nothing. He quickly shifted so he could ask Bridget about the other man.

She shifted, and Travis pulled her into his arms. She held on tight to Travis. "He's dead too. Heaton. This was Franklin, the man you killed."

The man had turned into his human form upon death.

"Hell, now we have to clean up the mess."

"What about Chet?"

They heard a van pull around to the carport, driving at the slowest rate of speed the driver could manage.

"That's the engine rumble I heard when I was getting you into your Durango."

"Did these guys have a third partner? And he was coming to pick up whatever he could at the house?"

"I don't know. Maybe. I only smelled the two men's scents, and Chuck only knew about them. They were going to burn your house. Heaton had a can of gas from your garage."

"Not any longer." Travis peeked out the blinds and watched for the driver to exit the van. On the side, a sign advertised the Christmas Tree Shoppe.

The driver's door opened and shut, but Travis couldn't see the driver yet.

Bridget shifted and put her paws on the windowsill to peek out.

Then Chet came around the back of the van and headed for the back door.

Travis took a relieved breath. "I can't believe he managed to drive that van anywhere on this ice."

Bridget purred in a cougar's rumbly way and raced off down the hallway. Travis hurried to throw on a pair of boxers, then ran for the backdoor to unlock it for Chet.

He glimpsed Bridget getting dressed in the guestroom, fastening her bra in front, and he was so glad she was okay, and hoped mentally she was fine after having to kill the other man.

He saw the naked blond-haired man lying next to the gas can Travis used for filling up his lawn mower. Then Travis headed for the back door and pulled it open, startling Chet who took a step back.

"Hell, I was going to shift and go through the door. Is Bridget with you?" Chet asked.

"Yeah, and Heaton and Franklin are dead."

"Is Bridget all right?" Chet asked.

"Yeah." At least physically.

Bridget joined the men. "I'm fine, thanks, Chet. You brought the men's van here?"

"Hell, yeah. I found you had discovered the men's home and had left with Travis. The men were gone. So I slipped in the back way, and confiscated their van to haul the drugs."

"And bodies. I think we need to take two vehicles. My Durango and the van. That way we can stay in our human forms and dump the van and then return here. Otherwise, one of us has to leave his clothes behind, which could incriminate us. I need to remove the rounds I hit Franklin with and dispose of the spent rounds." Travis returned to his bedroom, cleaned up the evidence in there, wrapped Franklin in his shower curtain, and hauled him into the living room.

"Do you want me to help you guys, or stay here and clean up the mess?" Bridget asked, already cleaning up some of the blood on the floor while Chet returned the gas can to the garage.

In truth, Travis didn't want her out of his sight. On the other hand, he'd rather she be here than with them if they got caught. "If you don't mind, why don't you clean up and if we have any trouble, we'll let you know. That could mean you taking your car and leaving the area."

She snorted. "In this weather?" But she nodded. "Okay. Keep in touch so I know when you're done."

Travis wasn't going to do it in front of Chet, but what the hell. He wanted Bridget to know that he wanted more between them. Something beyond this mission. He pulled her into his arms and kissed her on the mouth, his body pressing hotly against hers, his thoughts going back to when they'd hugged in the junipers near the rogue cougar's home in the freezing cold to warm her, and when they had killed their prey, shifted, and were both naked in the house. She seemed to want more too, which was the reason he took the chance, expecting her to push him away and scold him, if only for Chet's sake.

Instead, she held him tighter, her soft-sweater covered breasts pressed against his naked chest, her soft, sweet mouth kissing him back.

He should have been more circumspect. Instead, he was totally aroused.

She finally pulled free and said, "Be careful, the two of you."

Chet folded his arms. "No kiss goodbye for me?" He said it in a way that made Travis think Chet was teasing her.

"You might think more into it than I would want you to." But then she looked like she didn't want him to feel bad and gave him a quick peck on the cheek and smiled broadly.

"Jeez, one of these days, I'm going to be the one to get the hot she-cat."

Travis slapped him on the back. "Let me get dressed and I'll join you."

"*How* long have you known Travis?" Chet asked her.

"Long enough," she said, as Travis headed for the bedroom.

If he hadn't been getting ready to dump bodies and drugs, he would have been on top of the moon.

After he dressed, they got to the dark task at

hand and moved the bodies into the van while Bridget gathered more supplies to clean everything. Then both Travis and Chet tore open the plastic bags of drugs, the gravel-like granules spilling onto the van floor.

Because of the investigation Travis had done on Rambo already, he knew the man had two homes. The one was just perfect—out in the country, located near a pond, and no one lived there in the winter.

CHAPTER 5

"I'm keeping an open line between you and Chet so we all know what's going on if we run into any trouble," Travis said when they got on the road.

"How are the roads?" Bridget asked, pouring water into a bucket.

He hated that he had to leave her to clean up the bloody mess. But at least both men had died so quickly, their hearts had stopped pumping and the blood had stopped flowing. It was too bad they couldn't have just fed them their own drugs and let it look like an overdose.

"Roads are definitely icy."

"What exactly are you going to do with everything?"

"Drop them off at your friend's house."

"Rambo's?" She sounded shocked and pleased at the same time. "What...what if he catches you?"

"We'll be in deep trouble."

"Don't you dare get caught."

"We'll try our damnedest not to," Travis said. "As far as I know, he never uses it in the winter."

"So exactly where are we leaving the van?" Chet asked.

"Rambo's more remote residence. I know about it from when I investigated him before. It's not secure because it's not in his name and so he probably doesn't think anyone would learn of it."

"But it's really his."

"Yep." Travis wanted to ask Bridget how she was feeling about killing the man when she might never have had to do so before. At least when he'd mentioned if she could take down someone permanently, she hadn't said she already had done so. But he didn't want to ask with Chet listening in.

They had to drive so slow, he was afraid they'd never get to where they were going.

Bridget finally said, "I'm done. I'm going to take a shower, but I'll have the phone in there with me."

That reminded him of when she had taken a shower before at her hotel and she'd kept the line open and he'd listened to her sudsing up. He swore the next time she did, he wanted to be with her, soaping her himself.

His Durango slid on ice again, and he tightened his hands on the leather-covered steering wheel. "How are you doing back there, Chet?"

"Okay, just hope we're going to get there soon. Not really fond of all this ice."

"We're almost at the location." They drove on a graveled road, and then came to a large, frozen pond covered in a light layer of snow. "Okay, I need you to strip and give me your clothes and gun. Get back in the van, set the car in neutral, and send it down the bank into the pond. It doesn't matter if it doesn't sink all that deep in the pond. Shift and run as a cougar to the Durango. Then once you're in my vehicle, you can shift, and get dressed. If the snow wasn't already falling, no one would see anything but the van's tire tracks and cougar pugmarks. But with the snow starting to fall, it should cover all of them and the Durango's tire tracks completely by the time some concerned citizen makes the call to the police."

"Okay, let's do it."

Sweating it out, Travis went to the van and waited for Chet to give him his clothes and gun. Then once Chet did, Travis returned to the Durango, while Chet drove slowly across the grass to the pond. He kept driving it toward the frozen water when the hill had enough of a slope that Travis knew the van would continue to roll into the water without Chet's foot on the gas.

Travis said over the phone, "Get out now, Chet."

Chet ignored him and kept going until he was on the ice. He suddenly threw the door open, the sound of cracking ice filling the air. Chet shifted and leapt out onto the frozen pound as a cougar with his paws spread. Then he jumped for the shore as the van broke through the ice and began to sink into the pond.

Chet raced across the snowy, crunchy field toward the Durango.

"Hell, Chet," Travis said, pushing the door open for him. "I didn't say for you to go down with the van."

Chet jumped into the back seat and shifted, then began to get dressed as Travis hauled ass out of there.

"I had to make sure that it actually went into the pond so that it has enough time to dissolve the drugs. I opened the windows too so that the water would fill the van faster so no one can use the drugs if some criminal found it before the cops do. Though, I'm thinking if we have bad cop problem here, we might want to inform the DEA about it. Rambo could probably just say that someone else stole the van and killed the men, then dumped all of that here."

"Probably they'll believe it's some vigilante. Why else would anyone dispose of the men *and* the drugs. Still, if the DEA does any investigating to see if Rambo was involved, they'll learn his daughter was working for the dead men. Then the bodies are found on his property? He'll have some explaining to do no matter what."

"Bridget will be happy to learn that."

Travis smiled. "Yeah."

"Don't tell me you wouldn't have done the same thing if you had been driving the van."

"I probably would have gone farther out on the lake than you did before it sank."

Chet chuckled. "Yeah, you probably would have. You are always more of a daredevil than me. Now that we've taken out the bad guys—at least as far as the rogue cougars are concerned—our mission is done. I can put in a call to the DEA when I'm out of town tomorrow, using one of the men's cell phones. They had them and some ID in the van in a bag. Several IDs, I should say. I left everything in there, but one of their cells. I took the battery out as soon as I found it. I'll make the call and dump the phone somewhere on my way out of here. I can help you pack up your moving van, and I'll be on my way."

"Furniture is being picked up after Christmas. It's all from a rental store. I just have to load the boxes.

Do you have someplace to go for Christmas?"

"Yeah, believe it or not, I'm going to spend it with my widowed mother."

"Don't tell Bridget."

"Why not?"

"I don't know. Makes it sound like you're a helluva family man."

Chet laughed. "If you had family left, you'd be seeing them."

"Don't you want to wait until the weather clears up?"

"Nah. I think you and Bridget just might have something to build on, and I don't want to be in the way."

"She may want you to stay because of the bad weather."

"I'm not that foolhardy. I intend to stay at a hotel somewhere nearby."

"Thanks, Buddy."

"You'd do the same for me."

***

Bridget was so glad to see Chet and Travis pull into the garage, considering the weather conditions, and how many hours it had taken them to return. They'd kept her apprized the whole way back, but she still couldn't quit worrying—some because of the weather and some because of what they'd had to do.

"Chet said he'd help us load the boxes into the vehicle," Travis said. "Then he's going to a hotel and leaving in the morning to see his mother for Christmas."

"Will it be safe driving?" Bridget asked.

"I'll be heading south. Should get out of this before long," Chet said.

"I agree that we might as well pack it all up while we have more muscle." She had been surprised that Travis had included her as part of the equation. Like Chet, once the mission was taken care of, it was time for her to move on. But she really didn't want to move on.

"You don't want to have supper with us?" she asked Chet.

"No. I really need to get moving. Besides, I want to get as far away from here as I can and then put in the call tomorrow about the van in the frozen pond," Chet said.

"If you ever are down in my area, drop by and see me," Travis said as they loaded the boxes into the back of the Durango.

"I sure will. Got another case that's going to take me up north after the holidays though." Chet shook his hand and then offered his hand to Bridget.

She smiled and pulled him in for a warm hug. "Take care and be safe."

"You too, Bridget. I'll be seeing you around." Chet glanced at Travis. "Keep her safe."

Travis laughed. "It's a toss-up. Fifty-fifty."

Chet laughed, then headed out.

Travis pulled Bridget into his arms.

"Fifty-fifty," she said.

"Well, if we don't count you rescuing me from the Christmas Tree Shoppe. Do you want me to make supper?"

"My grandma always said life was too short. Eat dessert first." Bridget tilted her chin up, waiting for a kiss.

"Hell, I love your grandma. Mine always said to eat our vegetables before we could have dessert."

Bridget laughed and he leaned down and kissed her. His kiss was slow and deep and possessive. But her answering kiss was every bit as much as she licked and nipped at his mouth, then drew in a breath and kissed him deeply.

His hands slid down her side to her hips, pulling them against his, pressing his steel erection against her belly, proving the attraction between them was again escalating.

She'd never known a cougar like him where she couldn't read his thoughts, yet his actions revealed just what he was thinking, just where he wanted to go. As long as she was willing. And she was *very*

TERRY SPEAR

willing.

It wasn't just a primal lust between them either. It went deeper than that. The need to share the same space, to be with each other, to love and hold and talk to each other.

He slipped her sweater over her head and tossed it on top of the chest of drawers. She pulled up his shirt then, his hands molding to her breasts, the form-fitting silk the skimpiest of barriers, and she felt the heat of his hands searing her though the bra.

He was beautiful with his smattering of black chest hair trailing down to his jeans, his eyes darkened with desire, his sensuous mouth glistening from where she'd licked there. His hands slid up her arms and took hold of her bra straps. Then he slid them down her arms and kissed her mouth again. His voice was low and warm as he said, "You're a remarkable woman, Bridget Sinclair."

"You're not so bad yourself, Travis MacKay." Her blood was hot, her heart rate kicked up to triple time as he released her bra and slid it off her. Then his warm mouth trailed kisses down her throat to her right breast, and he licked and kissed the nipple.

She sucked in her breath, her hands in his hair, her body melting against his. He was solid muscle and hot, his mouth returning to hers before he began removing her jeans, and she worked on his belt.

84

Before long, she was wearing just her purple leopard panties, and he was wearing a pair of white boxers. He removed hers and then his own and swept her up in his arms. Then he placed her gently onto the bed. He prowled over her like a sleek, male cat until his naked body was covering hers.

"You want this? Me? Here? Now?" he asked.

She reached between them and cupped his balls. "What do you think?"

He smiled, his heated gaze taking in her very serious expression. "Good, because I was getting ready to beg, and I hate to beg."

They smiled and they kissed again.

He slid his finger in her tight sheath, and she purred in a growly, needy, big cat way, loving the intrusion, craving more. Their pheromones were flaring, kicking up the heat between them.

She couldn't have been gladder that she'd rescued the hot cougar, never imagining he'd be making the moves on her like this. Or that she would have been encouraging it.

His finger began to stroke her sensitive spot, tantalizing, drawing her up higher into a fever pitch of delicious torment.

"Need protection," he growled, his face a mask of barely controlled craving.

"We're covered," she said, breathlessly,

concentrating on his strokes, the way he could lift her up to the heavens. "Ohmigod, faster." Before he could rub her G-spot faster, she splintered into a million pieces, the climax washing over her in a state of bliss.

"Okay?" he asked, his voice rough and desperate.

She nodded. "Yes, yes. Go. Come. Do it."

He smiled, though his expression was tight with need. He inserted the head of his glorious cock between her feminine folds, pushing with restraint until he was all the way in and began to kiss her mouth again, his kiss gentle, loving.

"Oh, Travis," she said, kissing him back, her contractions stroking his erection, "so good. And so wickedly bad."

Travis smiled against Bridget's mouth, then thrust his tongue between her lips, and he stoked her tongue with his. She was beautiful as he began to pump into her, unable to just concentrate on the act of sex, but wanting more than just this with her. Her heels rested against his legs, her pelvis rising to meet this thrusts, and he came, driving into her until he was spent.

He rested against her for a moment. The cool air felt good against his hot body, and he just wanted to stay there claiming her like a male cat would a she-cat in his territory.

"Hmm," she said, wrapping her arms around him as if she were perfectly comfortable with him pinning her to the mattress.

"It's probably too soon to mention this, but, I sure don't want this to be a one-night deal with us."

"Good," she said, sleepily, smiling, her look tussled and sexy. "Because I was hoping you had more where that came from."

He moved off her and laid on his side, his hand stroking her soft belly, his expression serious. "Most assuredly. But I mean more than that."

They cuddled in bed, supper forgotten as he rubbed her arm, listening to the wind howling about the house when Travis got a text and smiled. "Chet's at a hotel, had supper, and wished us well."

"He's sweet. But he's not you."

"For which I'm truly thankful. And by the way, I accept your application to work with our field office in Yuma Town."

She smiled at him. "Oh yeah? When did I apply?"

"When you rescued me from the Christmas Tree Shoppe. It was the perfect test to see if you were cut out for the job. The on-the-job part of the application process had a perfect score."

"Ahh."

"We make a good team, undercover and

otherwise."

She smiled.

"We needed to hire more agents for the field office. And you'd be perfect. Better than perfect."

"Even though I'm a woman."

"That's what makes you so perfect."

She raised a brow, her mouth curving up a hint.

He tightened his hold on her and let out his breath. He wasn't about to let her go.

"So you want me to come work with your field office."

"With me. As a couple. An agent couple."

"All benefits?"

He smiled and kissed her. "The best benefits."

"So I keep you safe and you..."

"Keep you satisfied."

She laughed. "Ready for supper?"

When they went into the kitchen, they saw a sprig of mistletoe hanging in the entryway, the fragrance like the woodsy scent of pine trees. Bridget looked at Travis. "Did you—"

"Not me."

"Chet," they both said at the same time.

Bridget pulled Travis into her arms and said, "It's bad luck not to give in to tradition."

"I would never want to risk that. And I'm all for tradition."

They kissed, long and hard, then pulled away. "We'll have to thank Chet for his Christmas gift," she said.

"Agreed."

They cooked steaks, baked potatoes, and broccoli, and Travis poured wine into wine glasses.

"Yes, I left them out just to celebrate completing our mission." She could tell he was pondering why she didn't leave three glasses unpacked.

"You figured Chet would leave?" Travis asked.

"Let's just say I read his mind."

"You're good then. I was clueless."

She knew someday she'd have to tell Travis the truth if they continued to be close like this. She hoped it wouldn't be a problem between them. She was certain Chet had revealed his intentions to her on purpose because he kept thinking about how he was going to leave that night so she and Travis could have the time alone to get to know each other. She appreciated Chet for it. "So if I took the job, what would the living arrangements be?" She began cutting into her juicy steak, glad Travis liked his just as tender.

"We have an office-combo agent's house, two-story with three bedrooms, kitchen, two and a half baths, all newly renovated. Leyton Hill, the field office director, bought it. But for a time, if we want to stay there, we can. We have our offices in the main living area, kitchen, patio and gardens, the three bedrooms and two full baths upstairs. Leyton married Dr. Kate Parker and moved in with her this summer. Right now, he and I are the only two working there. He's the boss, so he hands out assignments, but he goes on just as many missions. Since I already closed on this house, we can buy our own place."

"Don't you think this is going a little too fast?"

"Hell, no. Will you take the job?"

She smiled. "I can ask if Chuck will give me a leave of absence to test it out. See if I'd like working for Leyton."

"You'll love working with him and with me."

She smiled. "No pressure, right? Okay, I'll do it. As for the house arrangement, we'll see. I have a home in Ely and—"

"Minnesota?"

"Yeah. Why?"

"One of our deputy sheriffs is from there. Stryker Hill. Do you know him?"

"Yeah. We dated. I can't believe he's in Yuma Town. A deputy sheriff? I figured he'd be in jail someday, not running it though."

Travis didn't look real happy about it.

"Don't worry. We dated, broke up, and—"

"You were going steady?"

She laughed. "As steady as fifteen-year-olds could be. He was wild, a cougar, and I liked that about him. But only when I was fifteen."

"He has a puppy," Travis said, morosely.

Bridget smiled. "I love puppies, but I doubt that would make me change my mind about him. We were two different people back then."

She mashed up her baked potato and topped it with butter, sour cream, and chives. She couldn't believe that Travis would worry about her with an old flame, even if that old flame was her heartthrob when she was only a teen. "So, what makes you think I might want to hook up with him?"

"He's a nice guy. He might have been wild in his youth, but he's a great deputy. And Leyton, our boss, should you decide to take the job with the field office in Yuma Town, is his twin brother. They only just learned of the connection."

"Omigod, that's so wonderful. I bet they're both thrilled."

"They're working on it. Stryker was kind of hopeful something might work out between him and Kate, the doc, but Leyton stole her heart."

"Oh. Poor Stryker." Bridget poked at her broccoli. "Well, I like the idea of working with you some more on covert operations. We'll just have to see how it will all work out."

They finished supper, cleaned up, and then headed for bed.

"So when will we leave here?" she asked.

"After the rental shop picks up the furniture."

"That means spending Christmas here." Bridget sighed. "I hadn't really thought much about where I'd be spending Christmas."

"Kind of sucks, doesn't it? No tree. No lights. No Christmas decorations. No presents to open."

They both glanced at the naughty elves and angels on the counter and the mistletoe in the kitchen entryway.

"You know, Christmas is all about the joy of sharing. That's it. You share your bed with me, since I packed your stuff in the bedding from the guestrooms and that works for me."

"You got me presents. I didn't get you anything," he said, kissing her all over again.

"We're good. Unless you insist on making it up to me later."

"I insist." He swept her up in his arms and carried her off to bed, and she knew the kind of present she wanted from him all over again.

It was dark and snowing, the wind still howling as Travis set her on the mattress. He flicked on the brass lamp next to the bed, but the light immediately went out and the room was plunged into blackness again.

CHAPTER 6

The ice and wind might have taken down electric lines and knocked out the power. Or it could be something more ominous.

"Guns or fur?" Bridget asked in a hushed voice, bolting from the bed and heading for the hallway. Normally, she wouldn't have asked. But since she had a veteran partner, she wanted to know which way he thought they should go.

"Guns," he whispered back. "If we have trouble, they'll be human. Most likely." He was leading the way.

She "listened" intently for any signs that anyone was thinking something close by. They'd have to be right outside, or she couldn't hear their thoughts, if anyone was out there. The wind was whipping about so wildly, it was wreaking havoc with their sensitive cougar hearing. She figured the only way to pinpoint if anyone was truly out there was to use her psychic senses.

Then she touched Travis's shoulder. "What if the lightbulb just burned out?"

He paused. "Shit."

She smiled, hoping that's all that had happened. But they couldn't risk it if someone had come to take them out. Maybe whoever ran down Travis's license plate numbers?

He moved away from her and whispered, "Flipping a switch on in the dining room to see if the electricity is really on in the house. Stay back."

She hesitated then, her gun ready.

She could barely make him out with her cat's night vision. If humans tried to break in and kill them in the dark, they'd have to use flashlights or night vision gear.

The sound of the light switch being flipped up caught her attention. No light.

"Moving to the front window to see if any security lights are on," he said, his voice hushed. "Stay where you are."

"Wait." She thought she caught the thoughts of someone by the front window.

Better be a big damn Christmas bonus for this,

the man thought.

"One by the living room window," she whispered to Travis.

Thankfully, Travis didn't ask her how come she believed that.

Someone crunched on ice on the back patio. "Back patio too. Do you have the castle doctrine in Wyoming?" With the cougars, they just had to terminate them. But with humans, they had to do this by the law.

"Yeah. We may use deadly force on intruders in defense of our person, property, or abode or to prevent injury to another."

"This should count. Too bad we have to let them break-in first. I hate to have to clean up all over again."

"You and me both. We don't need to shoot to kill. Just disable them nicely and then call the cops. As long as they're human, no problem."

"Okay, sounds good. What if we call the wrong cops? Or, what if these are the bad cops working for Rambo?" She still wished they could take care of this outside of the home.

"No one's warning us they're cops. They won't have a warrant."

The window broke in the back door and one of the front window panes at the same time.

"Damn it," Travis said under his breath.

Bridget was thinking Travis might forgo the use of subduing force and go for deadly now that he was going to have to replace windows.

The lock clicked open on the back door. "Getting him," she said to Travis.

"Got the one out front when he moves inside."

More glass breaking and then the two men rushed into the house, another following behind the one coming in the door.

She fired shots at both of them and both shouted curses and then she jumped behind the wall for cover.

Travis fired three shots in rapid succession in the direction of the front window and someone hit the floor with a grunt.

Travis moved back toward her, the other men breathing heavily, one holding his stomach, remaining in the dining room, the other starting to move into the living room.

No one said a word, but she listened to their thoughts. The man near the front window was thinking: *I'm going to die, damn it. I'm going to die.*

He repeated it as a mantra while the one man was in pain and was thinking: *Got to finish this before he kills me.*

She wondered if he meant them or Rambo, if he

was the one who hired them for the hit.

A cell phone vibrated in the man's pocket as he moved toward them. Humans wouldn't be able to hear the vibrating noise, but she and Travis did. Both fired at the sound, and the man cried out and went down.

The other stumbled toward the back door.

"Let him go or detain him?" She wasn't sure if they shot him inside, but if he died outside they'd still be all right.

"I'll take care of him. Be right back."

A smack, a man cried out, and a thud sounded as someone hit the floor.

She waited for Travis to return, not about to reveal her position if someone was still hoping to gun them down.

Someone was moving around and she remained quiet. Then someone started to move toward her. "Still there?" Travis asked.

Relief filled her. "Yeah. What do we do now?" Normally, she would have called her boss, but with a bunch of wounded men in the place, she couldn't tell him they'd taken down a bunch of humans.

"They're all tied up. Be right back."

She went to the bathroom to find a first aid kit she'd seen under the counter. She'd never expected to be using it to bandage attempted murderers' wounds.

Something clicked in the laundry room, and then the kitchen light came on. She suddenly felt vulnerable, like there were a hundred men out there ready to shoot up the place as soon as they saw them in the lighted room.

Travis quickly moved back into the hallway where she was waiting with the first aid kit. "Go ahead and bandage them up the best you can. I'm going to call it in."

She didn't ask who he was going to call. When one of the men lying on his belly smiled at her, his wrists tied behind his back, she figured he was with the police. Chills crept up her spine. She was used to having the military to back her up. She really felt out on a limb here.

"Yeah," Travis said in the bedroom. "Three half-dead men. The one might be dead by now. We heard them talking about getting rid of their middlemen, only the one said he'd lost control of the van and it ended up in the pond at Rambo Lancaster's country estate. Then they came here to take us out because we'd been investigating the two drug runners."

The man on the floor's face turned red. "What the hell is he talking about?"

This time Bridget smiled. "You know the old saying, 'My goose is cooked?' I'd say you're going to get to go to jail with some of the criminals you helped put away. Karma's a bitch, isn't it?" She shoved him onto his back and knelt down to bandage his wound. Looked like he could have hit the left kidney, but damage to the liver and stomach could have also occurred.

At least she was sure hoping these men were going down and this wouldn't all backfire on her and Travis. She hoped Chet was okay too, but she was afraid to call him and let these men know that someone else had been working with them on the case.

"Ambulances are coming and DEA agents are on the way," Travis said, rejoining her.

She finished bandaging the man, then went to check on the one by the window as Travis began bandaging the other man. The sounds of sirens filled the night, though everyone was slow in getting there because of the treacherous weather conditions.

The man she'd bandaged was wishing to hell he could kill the two of them and get out of here. He was thinking about how bad it would be if he landed in prison with a couple of drug dealers he'd put away, then taken the drugs off him, and turned them over to Rambo.

Travis unlocked the front door and opened it for the EMTs, the DEA agents swarming all over the place.

Travis identified himself. "This is my home and these men broke in there and there." He pointed to the front window and the dining room door. "We were just going to bed when I turned on the bedroom lamp and they cut the electricity. Because of the problem I'd had with the men at the Christmas Tree Shoppe, I figured these men were involved in the drug crimes also."

"We're police officers," one of the injured men said.

"Breaking into my house without identifying yourselves? Shutting off the electricity so you could shoot to kill?" Travis turned to the agent and said, "I filed a report and these must have been the officers who said they'd look into it. Instead, they kept the report of my being taken hostage secret. What did I know? I thought they were taking care of the men. But from what we heard them say tonight, they did take care of the two men who owned the shop. Permanently."

"Travis and I work for the same organization," Bridget said, giving her story. "He was lucky I was investigating Heaton and Franklin, and saw them take an unconscious man into the shop. When they left, I rescued him. I called about the case as we fled the scene, though I knew there were rumors a couple of the cops, at the very least, were dirty. Unfortunately, when we reported the case, the bad cops must have covered it up. Then they must have run down Travis's license plate number and located his home."

"What about this van?"

"We don't know anything about it but what one of these men said. We can't be sure who was talking. They were speaking about it outside the windows. They must have thought we had gone to sleep, and didn't realize we have combat training for our line of work."

"Just ran a check on you. Your boss, Chuck Warner, vouched for both of you. He also gave us some information about your work in the army. And yours too," the agent said to Travis. "The police chief and his department are cooperating fully with our investigation."

Another agent headed into the room. "We've got men who have found the break in the ice at the pond on Lancaster's property." He smiled. "We've waited a long time to connect him with his illegal dealings. The daughter's been arrested for complicity, and she's singing like a songbird. Apparently, she knows all the details of the drug sales and her father's protection scam. He had forced her to work at the Christmas Tree Shoppe, and she's willing to get amnesty to tell all."

"You know how this works," the agent said to Travis. "I know you're moving, but for the time being, this is a crime scene and we'll have to process the rooms. We'll need your guns also. You're free to go. I just need to know where you'll be staying for the next couple of days and when you leave here. We'll need your testimony also when the time comes."

They gave the agent their information and then headed to the bedroom.

"Because of the weather conditions, let's leave your car here and we'll take mine," Travis said to Bridget as he packed a bag, and Bridget grabbed hers. They bundled up before they walked into the garage, then climbed into the Durango.

They didn't say anything until they headed out on the road, driving slowly through the screen of white.

At the hotel, a Christmas tree stood out front all decorated in lights welcoming them. Bridget still felt tense and uneasy as if they were being followed or listening devices were all over their clothes and cell phones, just waiting for them to incriminate themselves.

"One room? Two rooms?" Travis asked as they parked.

"One room? Safety in numbers?"

"I love the way you think," Travis said.

But he didn't just get a regular room. He got the wedding suite, which featured a whirlpool tub, fireplace, king size bed, separate bathroom, wide screen TV on the wall, Christmas garland on the fireplace mantle, yellow rubber duckies wearing Santa hats and candy canes sitting on top of the folded towels.

He dropped their bags inside and started the fire in the fireplace. He was about to take Bridget's hand, but she quickly began digging something out of her purse. Two naughty elves and two angels. She set them on top of the garland, then she took his hand and kissed him lightly on the lips. "I don't know about you, but I've got to have a shower after what we just went through."

"Together or..."

She smiled. "Safety in numbers, remember? We don't have our guns now."

"But we have our teeth and claws."

"And together we are a powerful force to reckon with." All her instincts told her that he was the right one for her. Her match.

"I want you in my life for good, Bridget Sinclair. For better or for worse. I just wanted you to know that," he said, helping her out of her parka.

Her heart raced and she had to force herself to

breathe, staring up into his molten dark eyes. She had to tell him the truth about herself. If he couldn't live with it, she told herself that this strong connection she felt between them didn't matter. And she'd continue to work for Chuck Warner.

"I have to tell you something important," Bridget said, holding his hands, having to see his reaction. Not everyone would accept her abilities for what they were. And she couldn't help feeling apprehensive about this. "You might not want me in your life after I tell you about my...special talent."

He waited quietly, his expression tightening a bit, but he finally said, "Nothing will change my mind about you. About us."

"This might. I can read thoughts. Read people's minds." She expected him to frown at her. But instead he grinned.

She frowned at him then. "I'm serious."

He pulled her into a hard embrace. "Thank God for small miracles."

"I'm serious," she repeated, not understanding his reaction.

"I've been thinking how perfect we are together," he said, looking down at her like she was the most beautiful woman in the world to him.

"I can't read your thoughts."

He frowned.

"I don't need to. Your actions tell me everything you're thinking where I'm concerned."

"Then whose?"

"The men outside the house? That's how I located them. It was too stormy out to hear them otherwise."

"I wondered if you'd just heard a sound I'd missed. Does Chuck know about it?"

"Yes. But he leaves it up to me as to who I share with. Not everyone reacts in the way you did. Are you sure you're all right with it?"

"Hell, yeah. You're perfect for me in every way. I want to marry you, Bridget."

"I can't believe how you're taking this. Did Chet tell you?"

"No." Travis let out his breath. "When you rescued me and I learned you worked for the same agency, I knew we were a team."

She smiled. "You don't know how relieved I am that you feel that way." She was going to ask if he had any questions about it for her, but his cell rang, and she waited for him to answer it.

He pulled his cell phone out of his pocket and said, "Yeah, Leyton, hey, I've been busy, but I wanted to tell you I just hired a new agent for our field office. She's here with me now."

"In Cheyenne? She?"

"We finished packing so we'll be done right after Christmas."

"Well, I had a job for you, but—"

"Hold on. Let me put it on speaker."

"Ah, yeah," Leyton said, sounding tongue-tied all of a sudden. He never sounded that way.

"Bridget Sinclair, meet Leyton Hill, the director of the field office. And Leyton, Bridget, former CID agent in the army."

"Pleased to meet you," Leyton said.

"Likewise," Bridget said.

"So what do you have for us?" Travis asked.

"Since you've taken a break up there, if you have time between Christmas and New Year's, we've got a cougar shifter who opened up a murder-for-hire business in Las Vegas. He needs to go down before he can begin fulfilling contracts."

Bridget pulled off Travis's jacket and tossed it on a chair, then she began running water in the whirlpool tub.

Travis asked her, "You want to do it?"

"Las Vegas?" Bridget smiled.

Travis smiled back at her. "It's a deal. We've got some other business to take care of before we're off on the job."

"Yeah, sure, buddy. Hell, great job with recruiting a new agent for the office."

Travis watched Bridget do a striptease as she headed into the bathroom. He turned on the radio and smiled as the song was playing "It's Beginning to Look a Lot Like Christmas."

"She's just perfect. Talk later." Travis hung up on him and began to tear off his clothes.

"You didn't tell him you've been working all this time, taking down all kinds of bad guys," Bridget said, already naked, her dusky nipples rigid, her tongue sweeping over her lips making them wet for him. "Quick shower first, and then lazy time in the whirlpool?"

"There's not going to be anything lazy about the whirlpool time," he said, covering her breasts with his hands and massaging them. "But no, we can tell him later."

"Even about my rescuing you?"

"Especially about that. That's part of your application process, remember?"

Smiling, she kissed his lips, pressuring him to part them for her and then she plunged her tongue inside his mouth as his hands went down to her buttocks and pulled her tight against his aroused body.

"Anything else you want to do in Las Vegas while we're there?" she asked.

"How do you feel about dropping by one of

those wedding chapels when we get there?"

"Then I can make an honest man of you."

He laughed and moved her into the shower, not believing he could be this lucky to find a woman and an agent who set his world on fire even in the dead of winter. He began to run soap all over her wet body, getting his Christmas wish, that the next time, he was doing the sudsing. But Christmas Eve, they were going shopping for presents and Christmas Day, well, they'd wing that. Which was about par for the course when his sold house was a crime scene.

"I love you," he said, rubbing his body against hers like a big cat would, claiming her, covering her in his scent as her hands swept down his back, covering him in soapy water too.

Then he lifted her and she wrapped her legs around him. He dove into her wet sheath, no time for slow and easy with the bath water filling up the whirlpool, where they'd make love all over again.

"I love you," she breathed out as he came deep inside her.

And then they rinsed and quickly dried off, but he grabbed her up and carried her to the whirlpool bath just in time as "You're My Christmas Present" began to play.

"Next phase in seduction will be a lot slower, and much more thorough," he said, and set her in the tub and joined her.

EPILOGUE

Travis and Bridget finally arrived in Yuma Town ready for some rest after taking down the murder-for-hire cougar assassin and getting married in Las Vegas. They hadn't told anyone yet, but as soon as they opened the door to Leyton's field office, combination safe house, they were greeted by about forty cougar well-wishers.

They had presents for both of them for Christmas in an outpouring of love.

Bridget had never seen anything like it, and the way Travis's mouth hung agape, she knew he hadn't either. She read several of the cougars' thoughts— they already knew that they were married, but no one gave them a wedding present. She suspected it was because they were trying to let on they didn't know, so Christmas presents would have to do.

Leyton gave her a hug. "I want to welcome you to the field office," he said, all smiles.

She just stared at him, so startled that he looked so much like Stryker, she couldn't believe it. Then Stryker came forward and gave her a hug. She had to give Travis a warning look as she heard him growl a little under his breath. When she had dated Stryker, they'd only been young teens, for heaven's sake.

"We're married," Bridget said, "if you didn't know." She didn't want anyone to have to pretend they didn't know.

"Congratulations," were repeated all over the house.

"Hell," Leyton said, "I had to learn from Chuck that you cracked a mega case right before Christmas in Cheyenne. You should have told me. I would never have asked you go on the man hunt in Las Vegas and spend all the holidays fighting rogue cougars."

"We're a team," Travis said, pulling Bridget into his arms and kissing her. "And that's what we do."

"When you're not having fun with us," Dr. Kate said, squeezing Leyton's hand. "We are having a spectacular New Year's Eve party and celebration the next day. And it appears we're going to have to have a wedding celebration also."

Tracey and Hal Haverton said, "At the ranch."

And that was the beginning for the new special agent couple. Parties with the good guys, private time with each other, and missions to take down the bad guys.

"Love you," Bridget said to Travis, not having to hide how she felt about him in front of all the cougars present.

"Love you back," Travis said, openly kissing her and promising her their alone time was coming soon.

ABOUT THE AUTHOR

Bestselling and award-winning author **Terry Spear** has written over fifty paranormal romance novels and four medieval Highland historical romances. Her first werewolf romance, *Heart of the Wolf,* was named a 2008 *Publishers Weekly*'s Best Book of the Year, and her subsequent titles have garnered high praise and hit the *USA Today* bestseller list. A retired officer of the U.S. Army Reserves, Terry lives in Spring, Texas, where she is working on her next werewolf romance, continuing her new series about shapeshifting jaguars, and cougars, Highlanders, having fun with her young adult novels, and playing with her two Havanese puppies, Max and Tanner. For more information, please visit www.terryspear.com, or follow her on Twitter, @TerrySpear. She is also on Facebook at http://www.facebook.com/terry.spear. And on Wordpress at:

Terry Spear's Shifters
http://terryspear.wordpress.com

ALSO BY TERRY SPEAR

Heart of the Cougar Series: Cougar's Mate, Book

Call of the Cougar, Book 2

Taming the Wild Cougar, Book 3

Covert Cougar Christmas (Novella)

Double Cougar Trouble, Book 4

* * *

Heart of the Bear Series

Loving the White Bear, Book 1

* * *

The Highlanders Series: Winning the Highlander's

Heart, The Accidental Highland Hero, Highland Rake, Taming the Wild Highlander, The Highlander, Her Highland Hero, The Viking's Highland Lass, His Wild Highland Lass (Novella), Vexing the Highlander (Novella)

Other historical romances: Lady Caroline & the Egotistical Earl, A Ghost of a Chance at Love

* * *

Heart of the Wolf Series: Heart of the Wolf, Destiny of the Wolf, To Tempt the Wolf, Legend of the White Wolf, Seduced by the Wolf, Wolf Fever, Heart of the Highland Wolf, Dreaming of the Wolf, A SEAL in Wolf's Clothing, A Howl for a Highlander, A Highland Werewolf Wedding, A SEAL Wolf Christmas, Silence of the Wolf, Hero of a Highland Wolf, A Highland Wolf Christmas, A SEAL Wolf Hunting; A Silver Wolf Christmas, A SEAL Wolf in Too Deep, Alpha Wolf Need Not Apply, Billionaire in Wolf's Clothing, Between a Rock and a Hard Place (2017), White Wolf Christmas (2017), SEAL Wolf Undercover (2017)

SEAL Wolves: To Tempt the Wolf, A SEAL in Wolf's Clothing, A SEAL Wolf Christmas, A SEAL Wolf Hunting, A SEAL Wolf in Too Deep, SEAL Wolf Undercover (2017)

Silver Bros Wolves: Destiny of the Wolf, Wolf Fever, Dreaming of the Wolf, Silence of the Wolf, A Silver Wolf Christmas, Alpha Wolf Need Not Apply, Between a Rock and a Hard Place (2017)

White Wolves: Legend of the White Wolf, Dreaming of a White Wolf Christmas (2017)

Billionaire Wolves: Billionaire in Wolf's Clothing, Billionaire Wolf Christmas (2018)

Highland Wolves: Heart of the Highland Wolf, A Howl for a Highlander, A Highland Werewolf Wedding, Hero of a Highland Wolf, A Highland Wolf Christmas

* * *

Heart of the Jaguar Series: Savage Hunger, Jaguar Fever, Jaguar Hunt, Jaguar Pride, A Very Jaguar Christmas

* * *

Romantic Suspense: Deadly Fortunes, In the Dead of the Night, Relative Danger, Bound by Danger

* * *

Vampire romances: Killing the Bloodlust, Deadly Liaisons, Huntress for Hire, Forbidden Love

Vampire Novellas: Vampiric Calling, Siren's Lure, Seducing the Huntress

* * *

Futuristic/Science Fiction Romance: Galaxy Warrior

Other Romance: Exchanging Grooms, Marriage, Las Vegas Style

* * *

Teen/Young Adult/Fantasy Books

The World of Fae:

The Dark Fae, Book 1

The Deadly Fae, Book 2

The Winged Fae, Book 3

The Ancient Fae, Book 4

Dragon Fae, Book 5

Hawk Fae, Book 6

Phantom Fae, Book 7

Golden Fae, Book 8

Phantom Fae, Book 9

Falcon Fae (TBA)

The World of Elf:

The Shadow Elf

The Darkland Elf (TBA)

Blood Moon Series:

Kiss of the Vampire

The Vampire...In My Dreams

Demon Guardian Series:

The Trouble with Demons

Demon Trouble, Too

Demon Hunter (TBA)

Non-Series for Now:

Ghostly Liaisons

The Beast Within

Courtly Masquerade

Deidre's Secret

The Magic of Inherian:

The Scepter of Salvation

The Mage of Monrovia

Emerald Isle of Mists (TBA)

Excerpt from:

Double Cougar Trouble

Heart of the Cougar

Book 4

Terry Spear

PUBLISHED BY:

Terry Spear

Double Cougar Trouble
Copyright © 2016 by Terry Spear

Discover more about Terry Spear at:
http://www.terryspear.com/

Synopsis

Trouble doesn't always come in twos.

Jack Barrington still has an army obligation that takes him away from the woman who had enchanted him when they were both in college, but Dottie Hamilton refuses to marry a man in the military because of the problem of raising cougar shifter cubs in foreign lands and the worry he may be killed while overseas like her cousin was, leaving a wife and three little ones behind. When Jack returns home to see his family and Dottie's only living relative, her aunt, she convinces Dottie to bring her twins home to see her—and to see him. Jack has two-and-a-half weeks to convince Dottie to wait for him while he finishes his last three months on active duty. And learns the truth. Dottie's twins are his own flesh and blood.

Dottie has made a lot of mistakes in her life, including providing a father for her children by marrying a man, who turns out to be an arms' dealer. When Jack returns to her after finishing his army obligation, he's determined to prove he's the mate she needs in her life, and he has every intention of being the father to his four-year-old twins. Now the criminal deeds of Dottie's dead ex-husband have come back to haunt her. And she and Jack and their cougar friends will have to band together to stop the arms' dealers before they destroy what the cougars hold dear.

Dedication

This book is dedicated to Elizabeth Gaasenbeek. May your dreams come true in everything you do.

Prologue

5 years earlier, the Ozarks

Jack Barrington and Dottie Hamilton weren't looking for anything more than a hook-up when he'd met her at an Irish pub off-campus three months ago—a day of carefree fun, sex, and running as cougars through the Ozarks, nothing more. She was a pretty brunette with dark green eyes, a seductive smile, and a quick wit, but he'd just broken up with his fiancée and Dottie had broken up with a guy she'd been dating for two years. So really, they hadn't wanted to see this as anything more than a rebound.

Yet, that day had turned into several, then weeks, and then months. The more he was with her, the more he wanted to be with her...*more*. He didn't have any choice though. He was leaving, and she wasn't interested in being married to a man in the military.

She sighed as they sat at a picnic table and looked out at the forested trail that would lead them back to the parking lot, the road, and civilization. "So you'll be in the military, starting exactly...?"

"I graduate tomorrow and I'll be commissioned. Then I'll attend officer basic training and I'll serve at my first assignment. Not sure where I'll actually be until I'm at my course. What about you?"

"I have another year here before I finish up my degree. Then..." She shrugged. "I'll probably return to Yuma Town, Colorado where I grew up. All my friends still live there."

He knew he didn't have any future with her. Not when he had a five-year military obligation and she was dead set against marrying anyone in the military. She'd been furious with the previous guy she'd been dating for getting a bonus to join up with the navy without even telling her when he planned to just skip out on her. She'd broken up with him right after that.

Jack had even hinted that he would like to see her again when he could take a break. But she hadn't been interested. If her cousin hadn't died in Afghanistan, would she have felt any differently?

Still, he had to flat out ask. "I know this is quick, but, do you want to get married?"

She laughed. "No. If you could get a job in Yuma Town?" She sighed. "Want to run?"

"Yeah, let's do it." He knew he shouldn't have asked her to marry him, that she would say no, but he also knew if he hadn't asked her, he would have been kicking himself over it the whole time he was at the officer's course. He would just have to find someone who was fine with him being in the military. Someone who wasn't going to cheat on him. Someone he cared for like he cared for Dottie.

They stripped, stuffed their clothes in a bag and buried it under brush in the woods where they always hid it, shifted, then ran. He'd miss the time he'd spent with Dottie, and running in the wilderness as a cougar. He hoped he could do so wherever he was while he was in the military. Still, it wouldn't be the same as running with her. Despite knowing he really couldn't make a go of it with her—which was some of the reason she had said she wanted to be with him, just a flash in the pan fun time— he was feeling a hell of a lot more for her than he knew he should.

They'd run for about a mile, watching their surroundings, and he was watching her, when he saw a cougar move nearby in the woods, just a flash of tan fur, but he knew the male. Hellion Crichton—brother to Jack's former fiancée. If Hellion was out here in the woods so close to where they were, Jack suspected it wasn't coincidence. Dottie quickly stopped, watching the other cat, wary like Jack was. The guy didn't have a name like Hellion for nothing. Gigi was close to her brother, but Jack swore the guy was borderline psycho. As soon as the cougar leapt toward Dottie, Jack pounced on him, tearing into him, having to hurt him before Hellion hurt Dottie.

The two cats snarled, clawing at each other, biting, trying to take each other down. Jack wanted Dottie to return to the safety of his SUV, but she stayed there, watching, not getting involved. Which he was glad for. He bit Hellion hard on the leg, trying to break it to disable him enough to get him to quit fighting Jack. Hellion hissed in retaliation and leapt away before Jack could break a bone. Jack hesitated, thinking that Hellion might be ready to give up.

The cougar lunged again. Jack managed to tear at Hellion's neck. Hellion whipped around and bit Jack in the shoulder. Still, Jack was relentless, charging in, biting his opponent twice for every bite Hellion got in. Jack bit Hellion's bad leg again and that seemed to be enough punishment that the cat finally dashed away, his neck bloodied and he was running on three legs. Damn the guy.

Jack must have been a sight too. He was bleeding, though because of their faster healing abilities, he would heal up quickly. Just like Hellion would.

Jack and Dottie loped back to where they'd left their clothes, shifted, and dressed.

"What was that all about?" Dottie growled.

"That was Hellion, my former fiancée's brother. I don't know. Maybe Gigi is angry that I ended the relationship, thinking it was because of you."

"Oh, that's just great."

"Hell, I broke up with Gigi because she's been meeting up with three other guys and having sex with them while she was engaged to me! When I broke up with her, she was furious and said she was a free spirit. Free spirt, my ass. Calling off the engagement has nothing to do with you. We didn't even start dating until several weeks after Gigi and I broke up. Frankly, I didn't believe Gigi cared."

"And you're leaving tomorrow!" Dottie checked over his bite marks on his arms, shoulder, side, and neck. "The claw marks and bite marks aren't deep. You'll live. I'm driving, just in case you pass out though."

The adrenaline flooding his system, Jack felt wired and angry because the cat had gone after Dottie. "I'm not going to pass out."

Dottie narrowed her eyes at him. "You're leaving tomorrow! What if this psycho comes after me when you've left to join the military?"

She was right. What if Hellion did harass her, being the nutcase he was?

"I'm sorry." Jack didn't know what else to say. "I'd eliminate him if I could, just to make sure you'd be safe."

"Then you'd be a wanted criminal? And me a party to it? No thanks."

After half an hour of driving in silence, she parked near his apartment that was three doors down from hers, got out, slammed the door, and stalked off.

He couldn't blame her. Hellion was an ass, but he was also unpredictable. At the same time, Jack hadn't expected the guy to come after him either—or Dottie. And he had no intention of marrying Gigi if she couldn't even be faithful during their engagement. He hadn't been sure how his family would react when he had called it quits with her, but all of them had been glad. When they'd met Dottie, they were hopeful he'd marry her instead. Though he'd told them often enough that she wasn't interested in being an army wife.

At his apartment, he bandaged himself the best he could, called Gigi to tell her what her brother had done to him, thinking as close as she was to him, she could tell him to back off, but she only laughed. Hell, maybe she'd been the one to send her brother after him and Dottie. The thing of it was, Gigi hadn't even been broken up over their canceled engagement. Then again, why would she be? She was already seeing other guys. Angry with him? Yes. In tears at what she'd lost with him? No.

He really wondered if she hadn't cared until she learned *he* was seeing someone else.

After pelting down a couple of beers to numb the pain of his injuries, Jack tried calling Dottie. No answer. He figured she had to cool down. He really hated leaving the situation between them unresolved though.

He felt like hell, the bite wounds burning like crazy. He walked over to her place and knocked on the door. No answer. Not that he expected her to answer the door. Then he noticed her car was gone. He suspected she'd gone to stay with her Aunt Emily. He loved the woman and she was always trying to sway Dottie to marry him. Didn't work though. He thought of running over there, but Dottie had made her point clear. No on marriage. He couldn't get out of his service obligation anyway.

That night when he went to bed, he couldn't quit thinking of Dottie. He had to sleep. Tomorrow after graduation and the commissioning, the movers were coming. He'd stay with his parents that night, and then he was off to his training post. He shut his eyes and all he could see was Dottie's angry expression and it made him feel even worse about having to leave her behind.

***

Dottie packed a bag and headed over to her aunt's house. Hellion had terrified her and no way could she stay at her place if he came over to attack either Jack or her because she was seeing him. Even if Jack was leaving the next day. It didn't mean Hellion knew that.

Every time she became involved with a man, it turned out to be a disaster. She fought going over to see Jack though, to bandage him up. It was hard enough saying goodbye to him. She'd been on the verge of tears every time she thought about him leaving for good. She'd even been in denial about his leaving, trying to pretend the time they had together would go on forever.

This business with Hellion was something else. Jack should have told her he was leaving her alone with a nest of vipers!

When she arrived at her aunt's house, Aunt Emily tsked. "Jack is the best thing that ever happened to you. You love him, even if you choose to hide behind your cousin's death overseas and your last boyfriend joining the navy without any forewarning." Emily frowned at her. "Did you tell Jack about your dad?"

"No. Why should I?"

"Because that's the other reason you're so adamant about ending this with Jack."

Dottie let out her breath in a huff. "I never think of my dad. Ever. You should have seen the way Hellion came after me when Jack and I were running as cougars in the Ozarks tonight, and then Jack tore into him. I've never seen two cougars fighting. I was in shock. I wanted to leave, but I was afraid Jack might need me. And I was afraid to stay in the event Hellion came after me. I've never been so scared in my life. That's not something anyone ever taught me how to do. Fight, that is."

"So you're not going to Jack's graduation tomorrow?"

Dottie frowned at her aunt. What happened to any sympathy for Hellion coming after them? Her aunt had only one thing in mind. Jack was leaving and Dottie should be going with him.

If Dottie went to Jack's graduation, she'd want to see only him, and she'd want to kiss him goodbye and it would break her heart. Best to think of this as a fling like they originally had planned. If she could only forget all the good days and nights they'd had.

"I'm not going." Dottie was ready to move on with her life. Date? No. Just get her degree and return to Yuma Town.

***

The next afternoon after graduation, Jack was finishing up packing his personal items in his Jeep. The movers had loaded the rest of his furniture and boxed goods when Jack saw Hellion headed his way, murder in his black eyes, his neck and arms bandaged where Jack had bitten him. Jack didn't need to get into trouble right before he took off for his training. He wanted to call the police. Unless Hellion threatened him, he couldn't just call them. He had to see what the bastard would say.

Hellion continued to stalk toward him as if no one else existed. The three burly men who were closing up the truck, paused to see what would happen. Jack had his phone out, just in case.

Hellion pulled out a 9mm.

Well, hell.

Jack didn't have time to call anyone. He dove for Hellion, taking him down to the sidewalk, and yelled at the other men, "Call the police."

Jack didn't want to have to kill Hellion, just disable him, but he didn't want Hellion to kill any of them either.

"Yeah, a guy armed with a gun is threatening Second Lieutenant Barrington!" The mover quickly gave the address.

Between the hand-to-hand combat training Jack had in AROTC and the karate training he'd taken for years, earning a second-degree black belt, he shoved his hand against Hellion's nose. He heard it crunch just as Hellion fired off a round. The shot went wild and hit Jack's apartment window. A crack sounded behind Jack. *Damn it.* He was glad the round didn't hit him or anyone else though. He threw Hellion to the ground, wrestling with him for the gun. The bastard tried to aim the weapon at Jack.

Jack jumped up and kicked at Hellion's wrist with enough force with his pointed-toe cowboy boot, he heard a bone break in the man's wrist. Hellion howled in pain and lost the gun. If Hellion could have killed Jack right then and there, he would have. Putting one of their kind behind bars could be a real problem if Hellion decided to shift in captivity.

Hellion rolled over on his side and stretched out again for the gun. Sirens wailed in the distance, growing closer as they approached. Jack grabbed Hellion's good arm and flipped him over on his stomach, jerking his arm up against his back to force him to stay or Jack would break his arm.

"Can you kick the gun out of his reach?" Jack shouted to one of the men. He had a damn good hold on Hellion, but he didn't want to risk that the maniac would get loose. God, how he hated that he'd be leaving tomorrow, if he didn't get stuck going to a trial over this, and Dottie could be more at risk.

As soon as three police cars pulled up, the policemen got out of their vehicles and yelled at Jack to get on the ground, their weapons trained at him.

"He's the lieutenant," one of the movers said, motioning between Hellion and the gun. "That's the guy who had the gun and threatened to kill Lieutenant Barrington. It's over there. That guy shot the window instead of one of us because of the lieutenant's quick reaction."

"Hell, this guy is Hellion Crichton," one of the police officers said, taking charge of Hellion. "The store a couple of blocks over caught him on tape when he robbed the quick stop."

That wasn't good—not for being a cougar. Jack hoped If Hellion was found guilty and sentenced to jail, he never shifted while he was incarcerated.

"Hell of a job, lieutenant," one of the policemen said, shaking his hand. "I was in the Air Force."

"Thanks. I'll be on my way to more training tomorrow." Jack gave the police his statement. "Thanks for coming so quickly."

Then the police locked Hellion up in one of the squad cars and took off. Jack imagined the movers had never had so much excitement when moving household goods before. After they wished him luck and headed out, Jack called his apartment manager about the bullet hole in the kitchen window. He was glad Dottie hadn't been here to witness this.

Before he left the next day, he returned to Dottie's apartment one last time, just in case he could see her and say goodbye. Her car wasn't there. He called her aunt.

"Oh, my, she said she was going to a friend's graduation ceremony yesterday. I figured it was your graduation ceremony. She didn't see you? She's not here."

He let out his breath, wishing she'd come and congratulated him, or something.

He figured she would return to her apartment once he was gone. He hated the way they had ended their short-term relationship, despite the fact that neither had expected to have anything more than this.

Yet...he had wanted...more.